DIARY
OF A
VAMPIRE

KERA STONE

J . LEE

authorHOUSE®

AuthorHouse™ UK
1663 Liberty Drive
Bloomington, IN 47403 USA
www.authorhouse.co.uk
Phone: UK TFN: 0800 0148641 (Toll Free inside the UK)
UK Local: (02) 0369 56322 (+44 20 3695 6322 from outside the UK)

Published by AuthorHouse 07/18/2023

ISBN: 978-1-7283-7953-1 (sc)
ISBN: 978-1-7283-7954-8 (hc)
ISBN: 978-1-7283-7955-5 (e)

Print information available on the last page.

9 September 1846

To whomever finds this:

My name was Kera Stone, and I am writing this letter in hopes that someone can do what I could not. This is a dairy of my past and the events that led up to me being what I am now. I was able to find other passages from the other diaries that I added in an attempt to piece together the gaps. In this diary is the truth to what we are and how we came to be. I don't know if this will help, but my time is short, and I don't have long left. Somewhere down the road they lost their way—I think we all did—but I beg whoever is reading this to find the other diaries and use them to finally put an end to this war before it consumes everything. Save my friends; save us all.

—Kera

The Hell I Call Home

1 September 1836

My name was Kera Stone. I was born in England on 29 February 1820. Reading that date, you might be aware of its significance; I was born on what is known as leap day—a day that occurs only once every four years. To most this would be deemed incredibly lucky, fortunate even, almost a sign of good luck, but not for me. It was simply something else that could be used against me. Combine this date with the fact that I happened to be left-handed, and my personality was not what you might call *normal* amongst young women. The town very early on labelled me as a worshiper of the devil—a witch who was summoned here to curse the people of this town. Oh, if only that where true … the fun I could have had! But I was simply me, and I was not well liked.

Today is the 22nd of September, the weather is cold, the wind strong, and it is the year 1836, making me sixteen. My family and I live in the countryside in the middle of nowhere. Our family is quite poor; the only meagre income we get is from the crops and animals on my father's small farm. Last year's winter was particularly harsh, damaging the farm and killing of some of our livestock. Ever since that winter, we have struggled more than usual. Our home was already quite run down, an old barn house converted into a home, having barely survived the test of time. This year's winter has destroyed it almost completely. Our hand-built barn had been passed down through my father's side for generations, with every new one trying to keep it alive. Made from what are now decaying pieces of wood and old timber logs from the nearby forest, the shabby barn sits on top of a cliff that overlooks a never-ending deep sea.

The water is as clear as the sky, shimmering brightly in the light of the sun, and the waves create calming sounds as they gently move back and forth. The only window to the house is a small hole, jagged and curved, that looks like termites made it when eating their way in. Although, to be fair, most of the house looked that way.

I don't believe the barn ever looked new; it was always as if a small child had simply placed log on top of log, praying it would hold. It was just tall enough, however, to cram a second floor in, if you can call it that. Thin pieces of wood were nailed to either side of the house, creating the second level. The only way up is a makeshift ladder with wonky bits of broken wood nailed to the side. To this day I still do not understand how it holds, but I am grateful it does. Downstairs is just one big room, a kitchen tucked away in the corner that consists simply of one small wooden worktop and a large cooking pot over a small pit fire. Not far from that is a small, shabby table that can seat four at a squeeze. Finally, near the front of the barn, there is my father's space. It consists of one very old and chewed up armchair, but to him it is like a throne. It is a horrible, stained yellow-and-green colour, with a basic checked pattern. It sits facing the front door, as my father's logic is that people should acknowledge him upon entry. It isn't much; however, this little dying house of ours is home—at least for the others. But for me there is another place.

Situated not too far to the left of the house is our farm, where we grow potatoes and carrots as our crops. We also have a chicken pen with three chickens, one lonely cow for the milk, and a couple of horses for travel. A small fence encircles the farm, keeping the animals inside. It is the only thing that looks well done. Inside the fence, hiding away at the back, are the remains of what used to be a shelter for the animals. Long ago, before I was born, it was knocked down by a storm one night. Looking at it, it appears to be a heap of destroyed rubble. But what it looks like and what it is are two completely different things.

Over the years, I used this place as my escape and made it safe inside. It still looked unusable from the outside but that gave me my own secret hideout. The rubble had piled up to at least six feet high, so I created a pathway up to the top, simply rearranging the broken wood. At the very top lies one long piece of wood, the only thing that seems to have survived. On this is a large sheet of brown cloth that hangs in front of a makeshift window. Luckily the fallen shelter is on the edge of the cliff, meaning it has the most amazing view. I can see the deep blue ocean stretching out into the sun, feel the breeze on my face, and hear the sound of the waves and a sea that never seems to end. It shows a blue road to a whole other world.

On the other side of the cliff is the forest, which does not offer the same sense of tranquillity. We do not live in the town, and although our social standing is not high, we are classed as the working type, meaning we aren't at the bottom either. But because of the farm, we have to live outside of the town. The forest stands between us and the town of Mistill and is known as Mortem Forest. Its name was given to it long before anyone's memory. And, for good reason, its name is said to mean "death." This is no ordinary forest; it is so densely packed with trees that it is always dark in the woods; no light is ever allowed to creep in. The only guide is a small path made by travellers before us that leads to the town, but it is covered with sharp rocks and broken trees.

Town legend has it that the woods are haunted, snatched away by unseen monsters into the dark, and anyone who enters is lost to the forest for all of time. Because of this, another path to the town was carved out by men with axes not too long ago, creating a road. This path is lit by torches and big enough to fit a carriage. Out of the handful of men assigned to create it, only a few remain, and over time they have lost touch with reality. It is always guarded by the town guards, and only when permitted can it be used.

It is the only road connecting us to Mistill. One direction leads to our farm, another heads west towards the next town, and the rest the forest owns. As I mentioned, my popularity amongst the people is not great, so if ever I do have to venture to the town, I use the old forest path. Over time I learnt it well. The darkness of the forest, along with its icy cold breath numbing my body, is calming for me. At the end of the path is an opening to the back of the town, walled off over time. I loosened a few of the bricks and created my own entrance. This allows for me to slip in and out of town unnoticed for the most part—a problem my family never had.

My family consists of my mother and father, two older brothers, and my older sister, making me the youngest. My father is a small, stumpy man with no hair and a goatee. He hardly ever talks unless he is barking out orders to the rest of us. We never did get along from a young age, so my farther would simply pretend like I wasn't there, making me my mother's problem. She is a tall, slender woman with skinny fingers; long black hair; and dark, piercing brown eyes. She is obsessed with her social status; all that matters to her is being recognized and accepted by the higher class. My mother could tell this wasn't going to happen through me, owing to my many faults and looks, so all her attention has always gone to my sister. She is the opposite of my mother and me, pretty with long blonde hair and a petite build. Her face is perfectly proportioned, with blue eyes and rosy cheeks. She is perfect in my mother's eyes and those of the townspeople. Her personality, however, is as horrid as the plague. She will do anything to get what she wants, regardless of the consequences.

Then there are my two brothers. The eldest is very tall, about six feet three inches, with short brown hair and brown eyes. He is well built as a result of his many years of labouring. He does not have much of a personality; he simply follows orders and is a loyal, devoted son. He is already paired off to be married to the daughter of the local butcher. The other brother, the third youngest in the family, is not as tall or as big but can still manage just as well. He is different from the rest of them; he has always hated large crowds of people or having any attention drawn to him. This has made him shy and closed off and popular amongst the women. He is kind and caring in his own way but will always do as he is told. He is the only one in the family who has ever really spoken to me. My father can't stand me, as he sees me as a useless member of the family that does not contribute. My mother is disgusted by both my looks and personality and thinks it best to keep me hidden from the world so as not to embarrass her. To be fair, she is not completely wrong; the entire town thinks the same; compared to the other girls, I do not fit in.

My short black hair doesn't even reach my shoulders, and my pale complexion makes people see me as ghost. My only defining feature is my long legs. My whole body is slim, like a branch, and looks as if it could be easily snapped. My lips are a pale pink, my eyes a mix of green and grey with long eyelashes. My personality is different from those of the other girls; make-up, dresses, boys, proper etiquette—all the things to make a fine young lady—all seem so boring to me. It is a life I never wanted. My dream is to go on adventures, travel the never-ending sea, explore the world, be free to be whatever and whomever I choose, but it is only ever a dream.

The day I was born, my parents instantly thought I was wrong. Having been born early into the world, I was still fighting for my life weeks after arriving. My pale skin was never able to fully absorb the warmth of the sun, almost as if my body were rejecting it. As I grew and my features and personality became more noticeable to the town, I was quickly labelled as a freak from a young age—a worshiper of the devil, a witch sent by Satan himself—as how else could I be born on a leap day, a day that many considered to be full of superstition. This only fuelled the townspeople's theories about me further. My family agreed, and since I was little, I was cast aside by everyone. At first I felt so alone that I couldn't breathe, but now this void of loneliness shields me like a black coat protecting me from the world. Therefore, I lived there for many years, and it wasn't long before I realized I would always be alone. For the most part, my life was nothing more than a void, a black hole that seemed never to end. But every once in a while, in that rubble of a shelter, I would sit and stare out into the open sea. For a brief moment, I would close my eyes, feel the wind on my face, take in a deep breath of the ocean air and imagine flying over the sea, into the sun, and as far away from here as I could go. There would be this beautiful and bountiful woods on the other side, full of the colours of exotic flowers, noise from the animals, and the sound of waterfalls all around as the sun brought it to life. For those brief moments only, I was able to smile.

Through the Woods to the Town

3 September 1836

All the days seem to blend together now. Even when the sun and moon exchange places, I hardly notice any more. Everything is just one hollow movement through time as it gradually steals life from me. This diary is my way of talking to someone as no real person would ever want to. I wore hand-me-downs from my brothers and a long cloak that kept me covered, as Mother thought this would best as to hide me as much as possible. I simply moved from day to day with little care; still I had to do my part for the family if for no other reason than my own survival, so I was left with doing odd jobs and daily errands, such as cleaning and washing. For the most part, I was to stay home, out of sight out of mind, but occasionally my parents would be too busy to go to town, so I would be sent in their place to get supplies. This meant going through the forest of Mortem, although not by road. I took the same route every time I stepped into that forest. The small footpath winds through the trees. Chills run down my spine upon entering, my heart quickens, and I feel eyes on me always, but this does not scare me. My heart races with exhilaration at the thought that maybe something else is out there as the forest is deadly silent.

As the woods let in no light, I had to take a torch, which cast light only a few feet in front of me. Each tree seemed to have a hundred branches stemming from it of all different shapes and sizes, like long fingernails trying to hook and trap its prey in a cage. Sharp rocks littered the floor, with every couple of steps hindered by boulders or broken trees sometimes blocking the path. Bushes from the forest grew into the small trail, trying to cover it completely. There was no sound of wind, no rustling of the leaves. The forest was as silent as a grave. The only sounds I could hear from time to time were those of low whispers from the wind as though someone was trying to lure me off the path. The old path snaked through the forest, making it twice as long as the guarded path. It took hours to get through. After making my way through the trap-filled forest, dodging branches that seemed to reach for me, I finally emerged at the town. This forest path did not lead to the town entrance but instead to the small wall that surrounded it. Here I had managed to remove some of the stone and make an entrance of my own; this made it easier for me to hide from others.

The town is not large, but it is almost split into two. In the centre is the town hall, where the major lives; filling the rest of the town are houses cramped next to one another. Made of cobblestone, they are average houses—nothing special, but far nicer that what we have. None of them are any bigger than two floors, and all have the same basic layout: two rooms upstairs and two down. On the far side of the town are a couple of larger homes—three, to be exact. This is where the higher society live, each home at least three floors high and having a private garden. The town does not have a lot of shops, but there is a small market for the lower class, which is people in stalls selling what they can to one and another, and another area that was closed off to the peasantry, where the shops—such as the jewellers', barbers', and clothing stores—had their own buildings.

Owing to the rumours of the ever-disappearing townsfolk, the town council decided to build a wall not too long ago. The wall goes all round the town except for the road out. It is said there is a hidden path on this road that leads to the manor of the lord—a man shrouded in mystery, said to be a true gentleman that no average man could compare to. Although he had never been seen, his butler, on occasion, would be spotted in the town getting goods. He himself was quite the specimen, with a tall, slim build but still defined by his muscles; long black hair that he kept tied up in a ponytail; yellow eyes; long lashes; and the perfect young-looking face. He wore a black tailcoat and waistcoat, white shirt, and black trousers. The very manner in which he caried himself was to be admired. I did catch a glimpse of him once, and I could have sworn that for a moment he met my gaze.

I finished getting what I came for. Thanks to my cloak, no one knew who I was, so I was able to attend the market and buy what was needed with no hassle. On my way out, I noticed Tarell, a local tavern owner, standing by my exit while speaking with a hooded man. I knew better than to pry and moved on towards the town exit. There were always guards posted. Even covered by my cloak, I would be recognized by them at times, and they would have their fun by name-calling and throwing a few rocks, then letting me through. But today the guards had been drinking. As I came to the exit to leave, I waited for a chance to slip by and into the forest, but of one of the patrolling guards saw me. He grabbed me by the collar and dragged me to their camp, which was positioned a bit away from the town entrance, as if to be secluded. As he threw me in the centre of the camp like a hunter bagging its prize, I looked up to see the eyes of men—eyes that I knew all too well. I clutched my cloak as tightly as I could as the other three men grinned and headed towards me.

All the guards were basically the same; none of them had any defining features. All of them dressed in the same gear: plain brown trousers and long black coats covering whatever tattered shirts they were wearing. They all had scruffy facial hair and stunk of alcohol constantly, but there was one whose face I never forgot. The captain of the guards, Marcus, stood just above the average build, tall and strong. When he had you in his grasp, there was no getting free. I got to my feet quickly as he walked towards me, and before I knew it, I was pinned between him and the guard behind me. They were snickering and looking down on me. I knew what they wanted. Even if I was a freak, I was still a woman, and to the men of this town, that is good enough. I could feel the guard's breath from behind me on my neck as his hands started to slowly tighten around my waist.

Marcus pressed his body up against mine. Lifting my chin, he whispered gently in my ear. "You should try to enjoy this; I know I will."

As I tried to move free, the guard's grip on my waist tightened as he thrust me deeper into Marcus's body. In a desperate attempt to escape, I raised my arms to attack, but Marcus was much quicker. With one hand he grabbed both of my wrists, lifting my arms above my head, and the other he placed tightly around my neck. Gripping my neck tighter, he leaned in and ran his wet tongue up from my neck to my ear, nibbling at the end. The other guards stood and watched as if waiting for their turn. With every second, I felt Marcus's grip tighten and my body grow weaker. It felt disgusting, as though slugs were slipping all over me. I knew I couldn't physically outmuscle them, but I was smarter. I relaxed my body as Marcus's hand began to move slowly down my chest. The other guard released his grip enough to allow access to my front. I took a deep breath and waited for Marcus's hand to reach my lower abdomen. As his fingers crept down further, just before they could make contact, I tensed my body and simultaneously threw my head back into the guard behind me while brining my knee up into Marcus's groin. That got me free from their grasp, and I darted for the forest, leaving behind the items I had bought. The guards followed me towards the forest, but without a light I couldn't see where I was going, and I tripped and fell shortly after entering. Before I could compose myself, I was quickly pinned by two of them. They held my arms down as Marcus climbed on top of me as if he were straddling a horse, my face buried into the ground. He leaned into me and whispered, "We should pick up where we left off."

I was struggling desperately to breathe as Marcus's large hand tightened around my head and he pushed it further into the dirt. There was a foul taste of soil in my mouth. With his other hand, he began to rip my cloak off me piece by piece until only my shirt and trousers were left. The wind picked up, and the forest began to whisper. The two guards quickly got spooked, but I caught a glimpse of Marcus's eyes, which were open wide with excitement. I could see his lust and the animal inside of him; there was nothing that was going to make him let go of his prey. He continued to remove my clothes, easily ripping off my trousers, leaving only a baggy shirt to cover me. The tree branches swung back and forth like whips, scratching and pulling on the men. Rain began to pour down from the sky, and the forest grew louder. Afraid, the men holding my arms let go and urged Marcus to leave, but he madly grinned instead. He flipped me over to face him and made no attempt at securing my arms; he knew there was nothing I could do. As he began to slowly undo my shirt, in a desperate attempt to free myself, I swiped at his face with my hands. He dodged and slammed both of my wrists harshly to the forest floor. I thrashed desperately, but it simply made his grip tighter. I started to scream for him to let me go, but it seemed to encourage him more as he laughed. He went to undo the last button on my shirt, being careful to keep me slightly covered until the last moment. I was seconds from being stripped completely naked. He wore a grin on his face as he finally reached the last button. He took his time, and as the final button slowly came undone and he gripped my shirt, I closed my eyes tightly. Accepting what was to come next, I simply waited for the cold air to hit my naked body. But instead a loud scream echoed through the forest. Distracted, he loosened his grip. Using that small window of opportunity, I brought me knee up hard into his groin, knocking him off me and finally giving me chance to run.

Although there was no light, I knew this forest well, and even in the dark I was able to navigate it based on landmarks. I finally knew where I was and used the winding old path to my advantage. Marcus attempted to follow but was hindered over and over by the forest itself as the trees behind me attempted to block his path. I ran until my legs failed me. It was then that I realized the damage I had taken. The branches had lashed and torn at my arms; and the stones, my feet. Bruised and injured, I slowly limped home, hoping the state my body was in would be enough to please them.

I finally reached the clearing of the forest to my home. Hesitant, I didn't want to go any further. I knew what would happen if I were seen in this state, and the forest seemed the safer option. I had lost all the supplies and money given to me. My clothes where all but destroyed. I stuck to the forest edge and attempted to sneak into the barn unseen, but with no luck. My father and eldest brother, Darrel, were standing waiting for me. The second my eyes met with my father's, I saw the rage instantly build inside him, whilst my brother's eyes were different, like those of the guards. Like a bear, father swiped at my neck, grabbing me by the collar of my shirt. He dragged me from the barn into the house, where he threw me inside in front of my mother and sister. I knelt there waiting to be judged, waiting to be beaten as punishment for my mistake.

"You're a disgrace to this family!" he shouted. "You can't even do one simple task! It's bad enough that you look the way you do. No one will ever want you! You can't even contribute to this family—the family that feeds you, roofs you, and puts up with you!"

"I will gladly leave," I whispered under my breath.

"What did you say!" he snarled back.

I didn't answer. I couldn't. my whole body was shaking as the rest of my family simply judged silently. My sister was smirking the entire time, taking pleasure in my pain. My eldest brother, Darrel, stood with arms crossed by my father's side like the loyal dog he is. James wasn't there, so I guessed he was either working the field or in town.

"You think we want you!" he shouted. "We're family because we're connected by blood. We have no choice, and neither do you, so the least you can do is *be of use*!" He turned to my mother. "Can't you do anything with her?"

"Are you serious … look at her?" she replied. "Even if she didn't look like that and by some miracle I could do something, it wouldn't help given her personality. Even looks can't help her. She's too different; she doesn't fit in anywhere."

"Then maybe she doesn't belong anywhere," my sister suggested, smiling smugly.

To be honest, I didn't care. The idea of no longer being here seemed far more peaceful than the life I had now. Deep down I prayed that maybe they would finally end this.

"No," my father said. "Unfortunately, she is part of this family, and she will help one way or another. You will go without food for the next few days to make up for what you have lost."

"But I can't …" I began to say before he shouted back at me.

"I don't care! I don't care if all you do is clean up shit! You will work every day and be of some use! It's the least you can do for us having a mistake like you in the first place!" He then faced my brother. "Darrel, take her outside and sort out that wound on her arm. The last thing I need is her infecting us all."

"How did you even get such a wound?" hissed my mother. "A lady should be graceful enough at all times not to do something as stupid as cutting herself."

"I bet she was playing with the guards," said my sister in a gleeful tone. "News travels fast; Charlotte always sees her with them."

"Hm … so you have time to play around with men, but you can't even do a simple task such as bringing back food for this family. Very well, go back to town tomorrow and get the food you lost," ordered my father.

"But how will I without—"

"The guards are your friends, right? You seem very close to them. Surely they will help you. That way you won't be completely useless."

Darrel picked me up and dragged me outside and as far as he could from the house and told me to wait there. He returned shortly after with a cloth and some cold water. He told me to remove my shirt. I knew I had no choice, so I removed my shirt and placed my hands in a position to just cover myself. He slowly approached and began to wipe down my wounds. I stood there shivering in the cold, each wipe of the cloth like shards of ice piercing my skin. The reason I knew the look in the guards' eyes so well was because it was a look I had learnt over the years from my brother—the very same look he gave me once more at that moment. I turned around, as he never looked at me—a small blessing along with the fact that he would never actually enter me, violating as much as he could without being inside of me. It was always just enough for him to get his and enough for every inch of me to be touched. I kept my eyes shut as I felt his cold hands start to move mine away, exposing me. My body slumped down on to the dirty grass I took a deep breath and tried to be anywhere but where I was. After he was done, he simply said the same thing he always would.

"Mum and Dad might not think it, but I know you are a good sister who does what she's told."

He advised me to stay out of the house tonight, like a friendly warning. This had been my intent from the start. Night fell, and a blanket of blue and black covered the sky, bringing with it silence. James came to my little hideout, brining some food with him; he was the only one who knew it was there. I sat there silently, almost like a doll, while he placed it down beside me.

"I'm sorry, Kera," he said softly, unable to look at me.

"For what? You haven't done anything, so why are you apologizing?" I asked. "It's my fault. My fault for being the way I am, my fault … for everything."

He didn't reply. I don't think he knew what to say. As he went to climb down the ladders, he stopped and asked me a question.

"Does it help?"

My family never noticed—except for my eldest brother, of course. He saw the scars on my arms, as the brown sheet did not cover me fully.

"It's the only thing that does. Without it I think I would drown in the misery that is my life."

"You could run," he said

"Run where? Go where? Leaving this place doesn't change me. It doesn't change who I am. It simply replaces this place with another. The outcome will always be the same no matter where I go, because the problem isn't where I am, it's who I am. No matter how far I run or where I go, I can't escape myself." I sighed heavily. "I wish I were braver."

"Why?" he asked.

"Because if I were, then I would no longer have to suffer being here."

With that I turned away and waited for him to leave. Finally alone, I could do the one thing that granted me some kind of peace.

About six months ago, my father had left one of his blades on the field. I don't why or what I was going to do with it, but I took the blade. That same night, I stared at it for a while until finally I slowly lowered it to my wrist. The only logical thing that came to my mind was to punish myself. I felt that doing so would somehow justify what was going on. But as I started, it had another effect. The feel of the cold steel against my skin was pleasant. As I applied pressure to the blade, I moved it across my wrists slowly, deeply cutting them open inch by inch. Although I welcomed death—prayed for it even, at times—I wasn't suicidal, mostly because I was too afraid. I wasn't able to kill myself. Although if I cut too deep and was to bleed out, it would be welcome, so I just kept cutting deeper and deeper. The feeling was amazing, like a drug. Every time I cut was like a release of every bad thing, every worry, every problem in my life. For those few brief seconds, it all just went away and I was able to reach the surface of this crushing weight that I was drowning in and breathe.

This was not the only satisfaction that it gave; the blood dripping down my arm was punishment for me being me—a way to pay for my crimes. It gave me a sense of control where I had very little. Unfortunately this feeling lasted only as long as the cut, a few short seconds, so I did it again and again, and six months down the line, it became an addictive habit that I didn't know how to quit; nor did I want to quit. I felt as though it was my only lifeline and without it I would finally drown. The result has led to scarring up and down both arms. Some of them even carved as symbols. My parents have yet to see them, I think. Even if they were to, I doubt they would pay any attention. Luckily for me, the overgrown shirt I was wearing today saved me from the guards finding out. It would simply give the town another reason to hate me. I can already imagine the stories they would tell about it being some kind of blood ritual to the devil himself.

Hours later, I cleaned up as best I could. Not like it mattered; I was the only one who ever came up here, and no one was in a rush to get close to me unless he or she wanted something. I steered out at the sea, dreaming of a place far from here, and eventually closed my eyes to sleep.

CHARLOTTE AND THE LORD

4 SEPTEMBER 1836

I awoke to the sun's rays piercing my small window and straight through to me. The blood from the night before had dried on my wrists; it cracked every time I moved. I did my best to clean it up with some of the water used to feed the cow. Luckily James had brought me some of his spare clothes last night. Reluctantly, I headed to the house, ready to go back into the town. My mother was getting my sister ready at that time, as they, too, needed to go into town for a social meeting with a potential husband for her. In our town, arranged marriages are a way of combining the social status of one family with another to make them more important. Although my family lived outside the town, we still owned a farm and had some wealth to our name. A woman's beauty is also a way of measuring a man's importance; the more beautiful the woman, the greater the man.

In my sister's case, although her personality was like that of a troll, her looks resembled those of a princess. The only fault with her was her size, as she took after Father more than Mother; she was not as tall as the other women, but her beauty made up for it, as she was sought after by many different men. A week ago, my parents finally accepted a suitor for her to meet today—the son of the jewellery store owner, who was known to be of one of the higher social classes in town. Without my cloak, I had to use the brown sheet from my den as some kind of cover, but it did not work as well. As I got ready to leave, my sister couldn't help but wish me a heartful goodbye.

"Just think," my sister said. "Now it will be easier for the guards, even if you do look disgusting."

The weather was cold and bitter. Wearing such a thin sheet, I felt the harsh sting of each breeze with every breath I tried to take. Wrapping my own arms around me, I slowly made my way through the woods. Thanks to the trees standing so close together, they acted as a barrier, blocking out most of the wind's attacks. I did not rush to the town, as I still had not figured out how I was going to get the food without any money, let alone how I would even make it into or out of the town without my cloak. Although my face was covered, part of my legs and arms were on show. With my skin being as pale as it was, it was hard not to stand out. Walking into the town without anything to hide myself would be like willingly walking into a lion's mouth.

I knew I had no choice but to enter the town. There was no way of hiding myself fully, and if I didn't return with the food, the beating that would follow would be far worse than any whisper or stare. I simply put my head down and carried on to the market; it was like walking through a ghost town. All was so quiet except for the occasional chatter of a voice, and I felt on me the eyes of people that I couldn't see. By the time I had arrived at the market, the townspeople had figured out it was me, and the vendors refused to serve me. Be it through fear or hate, they began to shout. They wanted me away from their stalls, afraid I would taint their food or scare away their customers. They began to throw leftover and rotten food at me, shouting and screaming for me to leave. I didn't need to be told more than once, and I quickly darted away. I didn't even look where I was going, and in the chaos I ran into someone, knocking both of us down. As I recovered from the slight daze of the impact and stood back up, to my horror, I saw that the person on the floor was Charlotte. I found myself in front of the Tavern Maidens Kiss. Men began to come out to see what was going on as others began to gather. With Charlotte were two other girls—her followers. They did what they were told when they were told, and although they both looked nice, with long, brown hair; slim builds; and petite faces, they were nothing compared to her. Not only was she the major's daughter, giving her the highest social status in town with a pass to do whatever she wanted, but she was also the most beautiful woman in the town other than my sister. She had chestnut-brown smooth and silky hair that fell down to her knees, pale green eyes like faded emeralds that

16

drew one's gaze, full red lips like those of a rose, and a perfect body, standing tall, that every man desired. She was helped to her feet by the other two. She looked to see what had happened, and when she saw me, her expression turned fierce.

Charlotte loves a crowd and as much attention as she can get, so when she had finally composed herself, she made sure she was heard by everyone. This began to draw in the townsfolk, turning me into an attraction.

"You stupid little witch. Are you so dumb that you can't even *walk?*" she shouted.

I didn't speak. There wasn't any point. An apology would not make her stop, arguing back would not help me, and running away was not an option, because of the crowd that had formed. I had no choice but to listen.

"It's not like anybody even wants you in this town. I mean, it's bad enough I have to look at you, but for you to actually touch me ..." She scoffed. "My dress is ruined. How are you going to fix this?"

In all honesty, I had become so used to this over time that I began to stop listening and drifted off into my own little world of peace. I was quickly snapped back to reality by the stinging on my face as she slapped me as hard as she could, knocking me back down to the ground.

"Why are you even here?" she asked, standing over me. "Even a wild animal knows its place."

"Well, she *is* a whore," said Jasmine, one of the girls, from behind. "After all, you heard what happened with the guards, right?"

"That's right," said Charlotte. "I heard you went to go play with the guards. They must have been intoxicated to want to touch you. Or perhaps maybe under those baggy clothes there is something worth touching. Shall we have a look?"

I could tell from her expression what she was doing. Charlotte wasn't just attractive; she was clever, too, in a cunning way. Her intent was to strip me in front of the entire town. If she succeeded, then I would be humiliated; if she didn't, then she made the men curious, making me into a target. I shuffled back in an attempt to get away, but she had quickly grabbed my shirt. The other two girls came rushing to my side and held me by my arms as I sat defenceless. I don't know why

I screamed. I knew no one would come to my aid, but still, I didn't want to accept this.

As my cries grew louder, the crowd simply grew bigger. I shut my eyes as tight as I could. She had both her hands on my shirt, ready to pull at any moment. The crowd were dead silent in anticipation, almost as if collectively they were holding their breath. As Charlotte went to pull open my shirt, she was stopped by the sudden sound of a horse pulling a carriage behind it. She looked up behind her in disbelief as the other two girls let go and backed off. I was then able to see the cause of the interruption. It was a black carriage being pulled by two black stallions. I recognized the driver immediately; it was the lord's butler.

The town had fallen silent instantly. The lord was a bit of a mystery in the town, as no one had ever seen him. Normally the butler would come on foot; no one had ever seen the lord's carriage. Although no one had seen the lord, rumours were that he was so handsome that any woman who met him would be instantly charmed. Wrapped in mystery and wealth, he was the richest man in town and had connections with anyone that had any kind of influence, making him the most powerful man in town as well. The window of the carriage creaked open, and everyone held their breath in anticipation. In the shadows of the carriage, a pair of dark red eyes found mine. A cold shiver ran down my spine, and my heart quickened. I could not look away. In that moment, I was mesmerized; everything around me simply faded away, and the only thing left was him. The butler took a long black coat from inside the carriage, walked over to me, and offered his hand to help me up.

I brought myself to me feet, then he held out the coat as an offer. I looked back at the carriage to see that the window was now shut. I don't know why the lord would take interest in me, why he would give me something, or why he even knew I existed, but whatever the reason, it wouldn't be a good one. The people of this town had hundreds of reasons to hate me already; they didn't need another. I looked at the butler and shook my head, refusing the coat. As I turned to leave, my heart racing, still unable to understand what had just happened, the butler said something.

"Are you sure this is something you want to refuse?" he asked. "It may not be a wise decision."

"At least it's mine to make," I replied.

With that I used the lord's presence to my advantage and was able to move a bit more freely through the town and out the gates, knowing no one would dare cause any kind of commotion with him here.

I hadn't walked down the guarded path in so long. It felt strange and unsafe. I picked up my pace, hurrying home as fast as I could, longing for the dense trees in the forest. I got home, and my sister and mother were still in town. I knew that they would hear about the events of today and that when they got back, I would probably get beaten for what I had done. My father and brothers were working on the farm, so they didn't notice me come home. I quickly rushed to finish my chores for the day so I could leave the house, but I wasn't quick enough, and as I had thought, on my mother's return she was mad—but not as mad as my sister, who got to me first, striking me hard. After getting knocked down, I curled up into a ball and used my arms for protection as she took out her frustration on me, screaming with every hit.

"You stupid, good for nothing fool! Do you have any idea what you have done! Attacking Charlotte for no reason, then refusing the lord's hospitality as if you're too good for it, *for the whole town to see!* You have embarrassed me in front of everyone!"

As she went to hit me again, my mother prompted her to stop. She backed away, my blood dripping from her hands. Her face was red, her eyes full of rage.

My mother walked up to me slowly and looked down on me as she spoke calmly. "You truly are nothing more than a broken creature. There is nothing you can do right, and there is no one who will ever want you. Sometimes people take pity on broken things, and that's all the lord was doing."

I was sent outside and told not to enter the house under any circumstance, so I took refuge in my sanctuary. James came to me not long after.

"Why do you keep coming to me?" I asked.

"I want to help," he said.

"Help!" I scoffed. "Help how? You can't do anything, and it's not like you ever stopped them."

"I want to. I do. I just—"

"You're scared. Or maybe you just don't care. You don't come here for me or because you want to help; you come here for yourself, so you can justify what they're doing by telling yourself you're not the bad guy, just because you play big brother from time to time."

"That not true. I … …"

"Of course it is. I'm just a way of easing your conscience. But don't worry; you don't have to pretend any more. Just leave me alone, and don't bother me again."

"Why did you refuse the lord's help?" he asked as he went to go back into the house.

"Because nobody wants broken things," I replied with a tear falling down my cheek.

That night I did my usual ritual, but this time the cuts were far deeper, and they didn't grant the same release as before. Again and again I tried to feel that sense of release, but every time, the feeling became shorter and shorter, granting only a few brief seconds of peace. I cut like someone possessed, hoping I could do enough to bleed out and slip into a never-ending sleep. I chased that release until my arms became numb and covered in blood to the point that I couldn't even see the cuts any more and they felt heavy to lift. Thoughts went through my head that night, and I asked myself the same question I always do. Why was I here? For the first time in a long time, that night I cried until I was so exhausted I fell asleep, blood trickling from my arms and tears still streaming down my face. As I drifted off, I prayed the same prayer I do most nights—that I will not wake up and that this nightmare will finally end.

The Tavern Owner

5 September 1836

Maybe the devil really does know me. Only he could take a nightmare and somehow make it worse.

I woke to yet another day. I did not want to hear my name being called. Darrel had been sent to collect me on my father's behalf. I felt sure that after the events of yesterday I would die up here, probably of starvation. I headed outside to my father, who prompted me to follow him into the main house. As I entered behind him, I saw Mr Tarell sitting in my father's chair with a grin on his face. This man's very presence turned my skin white and frightened me to my very core. He was tall, handsome, and well defined, with short black hair that fell partly over his face, which had a deep, seductive tone and piercing blue eyes. Like a spider, his very presence would make my skin crawl. He wore a fine all-black suit with a red tie tucked into his coat. He was very attractive to others; for me personally, I just felt fear.

I looked around the house. It was empty. My mother and sister must have gone to town. I didn't see James on the farm, so my guess was that my father wanted the house empty for this visit. Mr Tarell was well known and popular amongst the men of the town. He had a reputation of showing them a good time at his tavern, with fine alcohol and the occasional women. He runs the tavern by himself but hires only attractive women to work there, so as to lure in the men and increase his business. However, there are vicious rumours surrounding the tavern. Mr Tarell holds a lot of power owing to the number of men he entertains. He knows everything about everyone, meaning he can do what he wants. It is rumoured that the women are simply given to the men as demanded and that Tarell keeps them on a tight leash. It is said the women have been seen covered in bruises and marks, and at night you can hear faint cries coming from the tavern. The most popular rumour that haunts that place is that of the missing girl who simply vanished one night. The townsfolk believe Tarell disposed of her for trying to escape, but a body was never found.

My father stood in the room, remaining silent, looking anywhere but at me and Tarell. Tarell got up from my father's chair and began to approach me. As he did, I found myself unable to move or even look away. He stopped only a few inches in front of me, leaned in, and whispered into my ear in a deep, assertive tone, "You now belong to me." He took a few steps back and continued to talk.

"It seems you put on quite the show the other day. The whole town can't stop talking about you. Not only did you attack poor Charlotte, but you refused the lord's hospitality. People are now afraid that the lord will be upset and take his anger out on them."

"I didn't—"

"Silence!" he snapped. "The people of this town have had enough. They want you out or they want you dead!" Tarell turned his attention to my father. "So I have a proposal for you, Mr Stone. I will take her."

"What do you mean?" asked my father.

"What I said. I will take her. She will come work at the tavern for me. The money she earns will be sent back here to you. The rest I will keep to cover her living expenses."

"Living?" I asked.

"Yes," Tarell answered. "You will live at the tavern indefinitely whilst working for me. It was an agreement made by the higher-ups of the town to put you in my care, where you can be of use. The alternative was death or exile."

"But how would she be of use? No one will go near her," stated Father.

"Don't worry about that; I have my ways. All I need is your consent, Mr Stone."

What about me? What about what I wanted? These people were talking about my life as if I were nothing more than a puppet on a string, deciding what I should do and where I should go. *Do I not get a choice? Am I not even allowed my own life any more?*

"Very well, take her," said my father

My heart sunk deep into my chest as I looked desperately at my father, hoping that maybe just this once he would show me kindness. He simply looked away. I moved my gaze to Tarell, who started to walk towards, me a devilish grin across his face.

"Why don't you go get your things so we can leave," he said, gloating as he gave my back a little push.

I headed to collect my things, the entire time in what seemed like a trance, waiting to wake up. There wasn't really anything for me to get; I didn't own anything other than the clothes on my back—nothing except for my blade. I looked at it for a few minutes and considered a different option until I heard footsteps approaching. Panting and out of breath, James stood at the entrance. I hid the blade within my clothes and went to leave. He simply stared, as if he were trying to find words that he couldn't say.

"I … I …" He tried desperately to speak.

"It's okay," I replied. "This is for the best. This way I am nobody's problem and everyone will be happy."

"Except you," he said.

"I don't think I am supposed to be happy. I think that maybe I was just a mistake that was never supposed to be, and that's why am not allowed a life. I never should have been born in the first place," I said, tears starting to fall down my cheeks.

"Kera …"

I wiped away the tears and took a deep breath. As I went to walk past him, he grabbed my arm.

"We can run," he said frantically. "I can keep you safe. We can go somewhere else … anywhere else—anywhere but here."

I placed my hand on his and removed his grip. "You still don't get it, do you? It doesn't matter where I go; this will always be my life. At least let me make the choice of not ruining yours."

With that I turned away and left him standing in the rubble. Tarell was waiting for me outside the house. My father was still inside. I took it he didn't feel the need to say goodbye. As I approached Tarell, he instructed me to follow as we headed towards the guarded path. I didn't look back. I took a deep breath and followed the devil down his road.

We had been walking for a while and were just over halfway, the journey the entire time having been silent, when I began to realize that we were getting closer and closer to the town. My brother's voice kept echoing in my head: "Run. Run! *Run!*" I took a deep breath and decided to try and escape. I started to look around for an opening in any of the trees but was unsuccessful. As we got closer to the town, I finally found a small gap that I knew I could fit through. I checked around me to ensure my path was clear, and I slowed my pace to quietly increase the gap between us. I waited until the gap was big enough to give me a few seconds' head start and took my chance. I quickly darted forwards as fast as I could. Too afraid to look back, I desperately reached my hands out to grab onto the trees and pull myself forward, but as my hands grasped the trunks, I felt his hands tightly squeeze my shoulders. My body froze with fear as I slowly turned my head to see him towering over me. I held on to the trees as hard as I could, trying to pull myself through. He pulled me back with such force it threw my body into the dirt. I didn't have time to catch my breath before he was standing over me. He removed his coat to reveal rope wrapped neatly down one of his arms. He slowly removed it, his eyes never straying from mine.

"I'm curious," he said as he continued to remove the rope. "What were you going to do after you ran? The town won't have you; that you already know. Your family clearly don't want you, and I doubt you would be able to survive on your own."

I didn't answer. I couldn't. He was right. Even if I were able to run away, what would I do next?

"Answer me."

I remained silent.

"Answer me," he repeated once more.

My heart began to race. I still could not answer his question, but I had a bad feeling about what was going to happen if I didn't.

A smirk appeared across his face. "Okay," he said as he began to creep closer. I wanted to run, but my whole body was frozen with fear. I could not pry my eyes away from his as he slowly went down to one knee.

"Turn over," he whispered in a deep voice.

I didn't respond.

He placed his hand softly onto my shoulder and forced my body to turn. It was enough to snap me out of my fear. I tried desperately to get to my feet, but his knee was already in my back and my arms were being pulled behind me.

Before I could do anything, I was lifted back to my feet with my hands bound behind my back, a bit of the rope acting as a lead. He placed one of his legs behind mine and pulled hard on the rope, tipping me back into his chest. With his other free hand, he tilted my chin up, our faces inches apart as he looked down on me. His very touch sent shivers through my entire body. It seemed that he noticed this as well.

"If you try that again, I will chain you up for days and punish you accordingly," he threatened softly with a smirk on his face. "I will make you scream until you can no longer speak."

He backed away, pushing me forward while keeping hold of the rope. As we continued onwards, he once again became silent. Only when we reached the town did he tell me to stop. He took off his coat and put it around me to hide the rope. Marcus was on guard. The second he saw me with Tarell, he made the connection immediately, and his eyes lit up. As he led me into town towards his tavern, people began to whisper.

The tavern was closed. Once inside, I could see this place was made for men. The air stunk of cigarettes and cologne. There where tables dotted all around the tavern, and one large private booth was closed off at the back. The bar was situated in front of the stairs, blocking them off, and overlooked the entire tavern. The place was of decent size and looked as if it could house at least twenty men, if not more. There was no style or fancy decoration to the place, just the bricks it was made out of and the plain wooden painted tables and matching chairs. He led me upstairs, where there where two rooms, one on either side of the hall. He pointed to the room on the left, telling me that would be my room. He then dragged me into the room on the right and said this was his room. He opened the door and threw me onto the bed, then locked the door behind him. His room was simple but elegant, decorated with red walls and black furniture. There were only a few things inside: a wardrobe that sat in the corner; a large bed as the centrepiece, resting against the wall with a small dresser next to it; and a desk in the other corner. There was an armchair at the foot of the bed, facing towards it, and I was curious as to why. There were no windows in the room, so it was lit by lamplight. Tarell lit the lamp next to the bed, undid his cufflinks, and began to roll up his sleeves. He walked over to me and took hold of the rope. Thinking we were about to move, I began to get up, only to be knocked back down. With ease he placed one hand on my chest, keeping my entire body pinned as the other wrapped the rope tightly around the bedposts on both ends, securing me tightly in the middle. Once I was secured, he sat on the armchair. Suddenly I realized why it was there and that I was not the first person to experience this. My guess was that this was how all of the girls working at the tavern were inducted, so to speak.

Tarell got comfortable, crossed his legs with his hand on his chin like a king seated upon a throne, and began to talk.

"I only have one rule: do as you're told. If you do that, then we will never have any problems. I will provide you with everything you need; all you have to do is listen to me. There are two other girls in the house who you will meet later, but I would recommend not getting too close with them. Distractions can lead to mistakes; mistakes will make me very unhappy."

By this point, I had given up all hope and no longer cared, so I suddenly got brave and decided to answer—a decision I wish I had not made. "Why should I care how you feel?" I muttered back.

I looked to gauge his reaction, and his eyes were wide with excitement. He slowly got up from the chair and came and sat beside me. His fingertips began to run slowly up my leg.

"I don't believe in torturing someone. I find pain to be a terrible motivator. Each person handles it differently. Some can withstand it until they die; others become so afraid they will do or say anything even if it isn't true simply to avoid it. Pain, if not used correctly, only promotes fear in others. This fear means they are more likely to flee or turn on you the first chance they get. However, pleasure … now that's different." His fingertips were now at my inner thighs. "Pleasure, true pleasure, grants you an experience like no other and leaves the body craving more." His hand moved up to my stomach, climbing further. "It makes you submissive and obedient. Granted, a little bit of pain is still good, as it helps to keep the individual in line. And besides," he said, slowly starting to wrap his hand around my neck and beginning to squeeze, "some people enjoy it."

All of my strength had left me, and I was unable to move as his grip tightened.

"I don't want to hurt you, so do not test my patience."

He released his grip and stood up. Seconds later, there was a knock at the door. He opened it, and there stood a very tall, scrawny-looking man. He was elderly, with grey hair, and was wearing a long black trench coat and glasses, and carrying what appeared to be a doctor's bag. They greeted one another, and then Tarell invited him in.

"Doctor, thank you for showing up on such short notice."

"My pleasure. I have wanted a go with this one for a long time," he replied, grinning at me from ear to ear.

"Unfortunately, I can't give you pleasure this time," Tarell sighed at me. "The doctor is going to make a few cosmetic changes to your face. By looking at you, I think your body is fine, but we will check. After all, no customer is going to want you as you are now."

"Wait, what do you mean, 'changes'?" I replied in a panicked voice.

"Don't worry, dear," the doctor said as he approached my bed. "I will give you something to help with the pain. I am not a monster, you know."

With that the doctor went into his bag and pulled out a syringe. I kicked and thrashed desperately, trying to break free.

"If you could please hold her still," said the doctor kindly.

Tarell tightly gripped both my ankles, making it almost impossible for me to move. The doctor pushed hard on my chest, restricting my movements. The events that followed that night where dark and bloody.

The injection knocked me out almost completely, but not fully. I could feel sharp bits of pain as I slid in and out of consciousness. There was a stinging sensation from my ears being sliced open, pain as my teeth were chiselled and filed down to a smaller size, and a pulling at my mouth as wire placed in some kind of machine was used to pull my teeth straight bit by bit. Small moles were sliced off my skin with a scalding blade; my face was tweezed, plucked, and poked; and the warmth of my own blood surrounded my head like a body of water. I don't know how long it took, but I eventually passed out completely. I awoke afterwards and felt cold; I had been stripped naked for inspection. It must have met Tarell's standards, as the only thing I felt after that was the cold steel of a blade as I was shaved from top to bottom. I slipped once again into a slumber, later waking up dizzy and disorientated, not knowing how long had passed. I could see the room was empty. My clothes had been replaced with an old nightgown, and the blood was gone. Exhausted, I tried to get off the bed, but I had no strength left in my body, and I fell to the floor.

Tarell returned and lifted me back onto the bed. He passed me a mirror, and I didn't recognize the person I saw. My ears no longer stuck out; my teeth were straight and white. My face looked young and healthy. Granted, it was still pale, but the tone was more like snow than that of someone ill. Even my lips where plumper; I had thin, stylish eyebrows and long black lashes.

"You look beautiful," Tarell said as he reached to take the mirror back. "Your body is in good condition, except for maybe a few missed meals. However, there was something I did find quite interesting."

He glanced at my arms, and I knew exactly what he was referring to.

"Those scars … How did you get them, exactly?"

I didn't answer.

"I will only ask one more time," he insisted.

I took a deep breath. "You know exactly how I got them."

"Why?"

"Why not?"

"Don't do it again," he warned me

"It's not exactly that easy to stop."

"I suggest you figure it out, because if not, what I do to you will be far worse."

Afterwards he told me to rest for a few hours and left the room. Still tired from what happened before, I didn't argue and almost instantly fell asleep.

CRUELTY OF MEN

7 SEPTEMBER 1836

I was woken by Tarell. I had spent the last two days asleep, recovering from my alterations. I crawled out of bed and struggled to my feet. I was still tired from what had happened and the pain from that night was still with me. From the neck up, it felt as if my head had been trampled by a horse. I took myself downstairs, to where Tarell was waiting with a bucket of water.

"The room behind me is a washroom. Use it to clean yourself up."

He walked me into the room behind him—if one could even call it that. It was a box with walls, painted all white and tiled, with a single drain in the middle. I could stretch out my arms and with my fingertips touch the opposing walls.

"This is where you will wash up before work. You get one bucket for yourself and one for your clothes," he explained

He handed me a change of clothes. It was the uniform for the tavern: brown cotton skirts that where frilled at the bottom, stopping above the knees, with a single thin, black line pattern going around them. Tucked into the skirts was a plain white blouse, fitted tightly around the bust. I was thankful to find it had long sleeves.

"Get ready," he demanded.

After what happened a few days ago, I had learnt not to argue. I got washed and changed as he went back outside. The water was not warm; it felt like ice.

"Wash up quickly. The other girls are waiting to meet you," he said from outside.

"Can't wait," I whispered slyly under my breath.

I heard the door open and suddenly felt a cold shiver down my spine, and it wasn't from the water. Tarell was standing inches behind me; I could feel his breath on the back of my neck.

"Do not make the mistake of thinking you are the first girl to challenge me. I have one rule in my house, remember?" he said as he drew closer to my ear. "Do as you are told."

He backed away and left the room, closing the door behind him. Once I was done, I patted myself down with the single cloth, small and damp, that was hooked onto a nail in the wall. I used it to dry myself as best I could before getting dressed. Tarell had also provided a pair of brown boots; they were shabby looking, with black laces and a little heel. The outfit also came with a thick black belt, which I assumed was to squeeze the waist and create a more alluring figure. As I was getting dressed, I began to realize that the chances of me escaping this place where growing smaller by the minute. I headed into the front, where there where two other girls already cleaning the tavern for this evening's service. Tarell called them over and introduced them.

The first of the two girls looked younger than me. She was small and very petite, almost like a doll, with long blonde hair, small pink lips, and pale blue eyes the colour of the sea. She was beautiful, but she looked as if she would break if one were to touch her. Her name was Teona, but she went by T. As we made eye contact, she smiled. It made her look even more innocent. She spoke very softly, saying hi to me almost like a child. It made me wonder how she would sound if she shouted.

The other girl, however, gave off a completely different vibe. She was taller than me at almost six feet. She was also slim but was toned, perhaps from the work. Unlike the small thing beside her, this girl seemed like should wouldn't go down without a fight. She had short brown hair, hazel eyes, and full red lips. Her name was Bethany, but she preferred "Beth." she was only just older than I. There was no hesitation in her voice, and she spoke with confidence when she gave her greeting. Tarell explained that Beth was in charge of us whilst he was away; I was to do as she instructed. After the introductions had taken place, Tarell explained the day-to-day duties at the tavern.

They were very straightforward. During the morning, the tavern was cleaned, barrels were brought up from the cellar, and the empty ones were removed. The tankards and tables were wiped down, and then we set up for the evening. After everything was done, we would have just enough time to eat before we opened up. Our food was leftovers from the markets; I could tell by the condition it was in. Tarell had informed me before opening that Beth would show me what to do and that I was to start today. He also told me that we were listen to the customers, sit with the customers, and accept any advances within reason. He continued to explain that no customer would dare to push his or her luck too far, so we had no reason to complain We were to serve, sit with, and entertain our guests until their pockets ran dry. After service, we would clean once again before bed.

Among the tables dotted around were a couple of small booths set against the wall with planks of wood nailed to them, creating small windows of privacy. The booth at the very back was completely blacked out; it had leather on the bench and stretched from one end of the tavern to the other. If it were any larger, it could be considered a small room. I asked Beth who it was for, and she said she didn't know; since she had been at the tavern, no one had ever used it or been allowed to use it, and she didn't want to ask why.

As the tavern was about to open, Tarell pulled me to one side and told me I was not to be touched by any of the customers; I was only to serve them drinks. If any customers were to try and touch me, he would handle it. I couldn't understand why I was given different instructions than the other girls. I shrugged it off as me being the new girl and thought it best not to question a good thing. As the tavern doors opened, I could hear the noise of the men outside, and as I looked at the faces of the other two girls, I saw both of them take deep breaths as if preparing for a fight they could not win.

The tavern opened and the shift started. I hoped I would be okay, but this place was a woman's worst nightmare. It was like being surrounded in the wild by a pack of hyenas, with each member wanting a piece of my flesh, circling me over and over, blocking all exits and closing in laughing, the entire time knowing that they would get what they wanted. Their eyes were always fixed on me, examining every inch of my body. Their hands were like snakes with the other girls, slowly slithering up and around them, securing their pray before they struck. Fortunately for me, no customer touched me. I assumed this was due to Tarell and couldn't help but feel relieved. However, the other two girls where not as fortunate. The men seemed hesitant, almost afraid, to touch Beth. T, however was never alone and always seemed to be surrounded, even though any of them could easily have handled her on their own.

Tarell would go from table to table, engaging with the men, probably collecting information or making deals. He would keep a close watch over us, and when the hyenas got to close to their prey, Tarell would warn them off. They could look, even somewhat touch, but they could not have the girls—at least not without his say-so.

When she got chance, Beth came to me and asked whether I was okay. I felt awful being asked that by someone who was going through a harder time than I was. She smiled at me, telling me that if I was able to feel bad for her, then I was doing okay. Curious about the situation, I asked her why Tarell was keeping the men in check. Her smile slowly faded, and she simply said, "Because they haven't paid for us." As I watched her walk away, I couldn't help but think of myself and wonder how many men I would have to serve in that way over time.

Towards the end of the night, as the tavern began to quiet down, a group of five men who had been enjoying T's company for the past few hours began to get brave. Beth saw this and headed towards T to help but was blocked by Tarell and told to see the remaining customers out. She stood there for a moment, face to face with him. After a few seconds, she moved to do as instructed. T let out a small shriek from behind Tarell. Beth's gaze met his once more with a fierce look. He smiled and called T over to him. The men let her go, and she stood by Tarell's side. He turned to face the men. He walked over to them. We couldn't hear what they were saying, but we saw them give Tarell money, and T's face quickly paled. As Tarell walked away from the men, he turned and loudly stated that they were to bring her back before sunrise in one piece. Shivering and scared, T was not able to move. Seeing this, I opened my mouth to protest, but at that moment Beth walked in front of us both. She told the men that T wasn't feeling well today and would be unable to accompany them. Although she stood tall, I could see how scared she was. Tarell stood quietly for a few moments as the men grew angry and began to voice their disapproval of the situation. Tarell then gave the men their money back and told them to leave. Not a single one argued back; instead, in a sulk, they were the last to leave the tavern.

Once the tavern was locked up, Tarell ordered me and T to go straight to bed. I looked at Beth as we headed upstairs. She turned to us both slowly and smiled before she was out of view. The room was very small. It simply contained three bedrolls—one for each of us—cramped into a box space.

Time passed, but Beth did not return to the room. I could swear I heard the faintest of screams through the night, but they were hard to make out. I longed for my blade that night, but Tarell must have found it when the doctor paid his visit and taken it from me. I thought it strange he never mentioned anything, but I guess he thought it wasn't worth it. I eventually fell asleep, and before I knew it, morning had come.

MY NEW HELL

8 SEPTEMBER 1836

The next morning, before we headed downstairs to work, I grabbed T and asked her where Beth was.

"Beth was the first girl here. She can handle herself. You would be better off worrying about yourself."

"What do you mean?"

"Tarell has never given anyone special treatment or told the men someone was off limits, meaning he has something special planned for you. If I were you, I would try and figure out why that is. She always tries to protect me because I look helpless, and I know that I am. Still, I wish that, just once, I could save her like she's always saving me. I must have been here for about seven months, and I have only ever been taken home by a single man twice; all the other times, Beth has protected me. She gets the customers too drunk to be able to purchase me or she drives them out. She's clever and is able to manipulate the situation. But yesterday was the first time I have ever seen her directly stand up to Tarell."

Her head sank low as a wave of guilt washed over her. We headed downstairs to start the day. On the way down, I noticed Tarell coming out of the cellar with a rag, wiping his hands. They were covered in blood, and his mouth was slowly dripping with it as if he had taken a bite out of something. He looked at me and T and said that Beth would not be working today. He walked away from the cellar and headed upstairs to clean up. Though I knew doing so was not wise, I headed towards the open cellar. T grabbed me immediately and tried to pull me back, but I easily broke free of her grip and continued onwards.

34

"Are you insane? What if he catches you!" she whispered frantically.

"She might be down there," I replied.

"Even if she is, what can you do? You're only going to share the same fate," she insisted.

"I won't be long; I just want to see if she's okay."

"Kera … Kera!" T called to me quietly. Her voice became fainter as I started to descend into the cellar.

When I got downstairs, I almost wished I hadn't. The sight that met me shook me to my very core, and it was in that moment that I truly understood the situation I was in. And I was terrified for my life. Chained up by both her arms, hanging from the ceiling, dangled what seemed to be a lifeless corpse, naked and beaten. She was bleeding from wounds all over her body, the blood slowly trickling down, creating a pool beneath her. As I approached to see whether she was still breathing, I heard T's voice from behind me.

"Is she alive?" T asked, her voice breaking.

I looked at her, unable to give an answer.

"Of course I am," a voice whispered. "I was just taking a nap."

I turned to see Beth smiling at T with blood still trickling down her face.

"Beth, I'm—" T began to say.

"Late. You both need to leave unless you want to join me," Beth stated.

We looked at each other shamefully as we began to leave the cellar. On our way out, I couldn't help but ask why. She told me it was punishment for her behaviour and saved me from the painful details. We left knowing that Tarell would be back at any minute. My guess was that the reason for Beth's punishment was to set an example as way of showing us what he is capable of. The only thing I could think was that if this was his idea of pain and fear, I had no clue what his idea of pleasure might be.

After the tavern opened that night with Beth gone, T received more advances than usual and was badly harassed by the men. I noticed that Tarell was smiling throughout the night. With Beth gone, there was no one there to protect us. The same five men from the night before came back as we were closing, making the same offer to Tarell for T. Tarell once again agreed, and this time there was no one to stop him. I wanted to help, but all I could imagine was Beth's beaten and chained-up body and how that would be me. All I could do was watch as they took her away. I was told to lock up the tavern shortly after they left as Tarell headed to his room. As I did, I could hear noises coming from outside. I slowly crept round the corner of the tavern to see the men with T; she had been backed into a corner and was surrounded. I didn't want to be a coward twice, but I also wasn't stupid. I slowly sneaked behind them, picking up a rock as I approached. In a desperate attempt to help, with all my strength I hit one of them as hard as I could in the back of the head, and in the confusion I was able to grab T's arm and pull her away from the group. We ran as fast as we could, aiming for the tavern, but it took only seconds for one of them to snatch T away from me and throw her back into the wall hard. She let out a yelp of pain and quickly fell to the floor. Suddenly they were no longer interested in her; all of their attention turned to me, and all I could see was the rage in their eyes. I began to back away carefully as they moved closer step by step. I attempted to turn and flee, but it was no use. Before I knew it, I was once again pinned to the floor, powerless, staring up at their greedy faces.

I looked over at T as she tried to get to her feet. She looked at me, and I shook my head to tell her to stay down. We couldn't fight back, and we couldn't run, but we didn't both have to suffer. With their attention fixated on me, I hoped, they would leave her be. I closed my eyes and tried to relax my body to reduce the pain as much as possible. All I could hear was laughter and the sound of belts coming undone. I imagined myself on the cliff edge overlooking the never-ending sea, but I still couldn't stop the tears that slowly fell from my eyes.

Suddenly it was silent. The grip on my arms had gone. I thought perhaps I had died from the shock, but when I opened my eyes, the men were gone. I looked over at T to see her in the arms of the lord's butler, unconscious—passed out from the shock, I assumed. As I looked back, a tall, dark figure stood over me. I saw the lord's face up close for the first time. The rumours did not do him justice; this man was not just handsome; his very presence shouted power. Like an alpha wolf, he stood tall and strong. His eyes were black with a tint of yellow; he had short black hair, and stubble covered his beautifully structured face. He was built well—I could easily see the muscles through his clothes—but not so much so as to seem overpowering. His was the perfect balance of power and elegance. This man was a sight to behold in many different ways. Unlike other men whose gazes I had met previously, I did not feel trapped or scared, but almost instantly safe—a feeling I had not felt for as long as I could remember.

He offered his hand, and without thinking, I took it. He helped me to my feet. He then spoke to me for the first time, his voice deep and calming.

"Are you okay, milady?" he asked

"The men," I muttered.

"They're gone. I don't see them coming back," he asserted. "You're working at the tavern. Was this by choice, may I ask?"

"Not exactly."

"Hmm. As I thought. Allow me to accompany you inside. My butler will take this young lady back to her room."

I wasn't able to reply. No one had ever asked me whether anything was okay with me. He smiled and began to lead me inside. His smile was as beautiful as him. It was genuine; there was no malice behind it. We went inside.

Tarell was downstairs waiting. I assumed he had heard everything, but to my surprise he was not mad. If anything, he seemed almost happy. I noticed that the cellar door was locked and there were faint spots of blood leading upstairs. My guess was that he moved Beth during the commotion to save face in front of the lord. The butler ushered me to follow him upstairs as the lord went to go talk with Tarell.

"Goodnight, Miss Stone. I hope to see you again soon."

As we got upstairs, the butler gently placed T onto her bed and checked her over, treating any wounds. He told me there were no internal injuries, but she would need bed rest for a few days. He continued to say he would advise Tarell to keep her rested for now. As he went to leave, I stopped him and asked him why no one had ever seen the lord and he had never before interfered with the affairs of the townspeople. "It's not like I am the first or the only victim in this town, so why? Why help me?"

"First you don't accept his help; now you question it," he answered.

I realized he was talking about the incident with Charlotte.

"A kind gesture can sometimes do more bad than good. The lord's small gestures are only going to bring more attention to me and probably make things worse. The only person who can save you is yourself, and I don't see that happening."

"And what if he was to save you?" the butler asked.

Why would he? I thought. There was no reason that came to mind that would explain why the lord would want to save someone like me. All people had ever done was use and abuse me my entire life. He seemed kinder, but experience showed that in the end they are all the same.

"Miss Stone, you shouldn't assume that all people are the same, though I can understand why you might. But even out of a thousand, you need only one good one to reach out a hand."

"And you are telling me the lord is that one good man?"

"That is something you will have to find out for yourself, if you want to."

With that he bowed politely to me and left. As I heard him reach the bottom of the stairs, the bedroom door opened once again. Beth was standing there, cleaned up but still covered in bruises, struggling to move. She came in and sat beside T. I caught her up on the events. I was expecting questions—and a lot of them—but instead she simply let out a sigh of relief and said, "Thank God you are both okay." As she didn't ask me any questions, I granted her the same courtesy. It wasn't long before she fell asleep next to T, but I was not able to do the same; there was so much going on in my head that just didn't make sense.

The more I thought about it, the more anxious I got and the more theories I developed. *What if the lord is working for Tarell? What if it's a trap to gain our trust? What if he wants us for his company? What if...?* The ideas kept coming until I found myself sitting rocking with my knees tight to my chest. This continued for what seemed like most of the night. Remembering that Tarell and the lord had left early that night, I sneaked downstairs into the back storage room, where Tarell kept items for the tavern, and was able to find a knife. I took the knife and, without hesitation, where I stood, sliced my wrist. As I did, I felt the release as all my emotions left my body. In a moment of bliss, I closed my eyes and felt at peace. As I opened them, the emotions began to return, so I repeated the process over and over until I felt a cold hand stop me.

Tarell was standing in front of me. I hadn't even heard him enter the tavern. He gently took my wrist and guided me to the washroom. He left me there as he went to get some water. I hadn't realized how much I had done, but I began to feel dizzy from the blood loss. As I looked down, I realized my arms were cut all the way up to my elbow, gash after gash. He came back and very gently cleaned up the wounds, but the bleeding would not stop. He let out a sigh and reached for the blade clutched in my fingers. He smiled at me and then, without hesitation, began to cut into my arm over the wounds I had made. The shock took me by surprise, and I fell instantly to my knees. He repeated the process over and over until there was no longer any discernible pattern to them.

"I spend all that money and time making you into this beautiful young lady, and you go and repay me by damaging my property," he said calmly as he put the knife down and once again began to clean my wounds. "I don't know if it's because you want to die or because you get some kind of thrill out of it, but I don't care; you are not to do it again."

"Then why add to them?" I asked, barely able to speak, as I could feel myself passing out.

"Because now we can say you were attacked by a wild animal, meaning you can still be of use. But if this happens again, then maybe that wild animal did more harm than just a few scratches," he said, bending down to my level and getting close to my face. "Maybe next time it takes your entire arm."

He finished cleaning me up and tied a rag around my wrist to stop the bleeding. He then pulled to my feet and ushered me back upstairs to bed.

"Besides," he said as I crawled up the stairs, "you may not care much for your own health, but you do seem to care for theirs. I warned you getting close to them was not a good idea."

He didn't have to say anything else. I knew that if I made a mistake again, it would not be me who would suffer his wrath. I got upstairs and stumbled into my bed. Maybe it was due to the events of the day or the amount of blood I had lost, but I was quickly asleep. No dreams, no thoughts—just swept away by the calmness of nothing.

FROM ONE CAPTOR TO ANOTHER

9 SEPTEMBER 1836

That morning as I awoke, I saw Beth and T tending to my wrist with water and a cloth. They didn't ask about my wrists. Instead T just smiled at me and said, "We all have our own way of managing in life, but that doesn't mean we have to do it alone."

"If you are willing to help someone else, then you should be willing to receive help as well." As Beth said this, I couldn't help but feel as though this wasn't the first time she had done this. There was so much pain in her eyes, but she never showed it on her face. I envied her in that moment and wished that I had the same strength.

In the afternoon, we started work as normal, but everything was about to change. As it grew late into the night, the lord entered the tavern and Tarell directed him to the huge booth at the back. The atmosphere of the tavern changed. No one dared to say a thing, drink, or even move; it fell deadly silent. After a while, whispers began to emerge on speculation of what he was doing. He didn't order a drink or request anything; he simply sat in the booth. With him there, no one dared to touch the girls. Despite the booths being private, it was as if his gaze were on everyone at all times—watching, waiting. This continued for the rest of the night, slowly driving the rest of the men out. I thought Tarell would be annoyed and force him out for causing the customers to leave, but instead he seemed happier than ever. Like a sly fox planning his next move, he stood silently watching. At the end of the night, when the tavern had emptied except for the lord, an unexpected guest visited. My brother James walked into the tavern, tired and panting as if he had run form the house. James was a big guy himself and was hard to intimidate. He began to walk towards me until his path was blocked by Tarell. Although my brother was bigger, Tarell was not intimidated; nor did he have any intent of moving. They stood toe to toe, neither one backing down.

"She isn't staying here any longer. No matter the price, I will pay it, but she leaves with me now!" my brother demanded.

"I am afraid there is no price you could offer me that will compensate me losing her. And a deal was struck with your father. You have no claim to her, boy," he snarled.

"She's my *sister!*" he shouted.

With that James grabbed Tarell by the front of his shirt and threatened that he let me go. From behind, the lord appeared out of his booth and placed his hand on James's shoulder, removing his grip from Tarell. "You must love your sister very much to fight for her, but Tarell is right; there is nothing you can do," the lord calmy explained.

"But—" James began to argue.

"However, maybe we can come to an arrangement, Mr Tarell?" suggested the lord.

"What do you have in mind?" he asked.

They were just talking about me as if I wasn't here, as if I wasn't real, wasn't a person with feelings or a will of my own. What about what I wanted? What about my choices? It was my life; why didn't I get to decide?

"It's my *liiiiiiiiiiife!*" I shouted at the top of my lungs.

The room fell silent as everyone looked upon me. I stood there panting, shaking, scared, and angry at the same time, my fists clenched. I didn't know what I was doing; I just knew I wanted to choose for myself.

"You all stand there and talk as if I'm an object. I know I am hardly worth anything, but It's my life, and I want to choose what I do."

I felt a mix of emotions ranging from shock to anger, from disbelief to fear, as I looked each one of them in the eye. I stood firm, ready to accept what came next.

"How about I offer you the choice then," said the lord, turning to face me. "Come with me to my manor for one month and live under my care. Of course, the other girls can come too. At the end of the month, there will be a ball. After the ball, if you decide to leave my care, I will not stop you, and I will provide you with what you need to start a new life. However, if you decide to stay, then you will stay as my guest. In the meantime, while you are there, you will be expected to work in the house. Mr Tarell, I assume this is okay with you. Of course I will cover any losses over that month, plus a bit on interest as a sign of good faith."

For a moment, Tarell did not answer; he looked at me, and the other girls then turned back to the lord.

"I have no issue with you taking her," he finally replied, "but only her. And after the month is up, if you wish to keep her, a new agreement must be made. I will attend the ball to see the outcome for myself. I assume I am invited, of course."

"No, she doesn't need any of that. She's coming home with me now!" declared James.

I realized that at this moment, although it wasn't much, I had a bit of control and was able to decide for myself and, if I were lucky, the girls as well. Due to the amount of effort the lord had put in so far, I gambled that he wasn't taking no for an answer and used that to my advantage.

"Here is my offer," I asserted, "and the only one I will accept. I will go with the lord and take one of the girls with me. The other girl who remains here is not to be touched at all or given to any man. The lord will compensate for any financial losses. I won't go anywhere if they are at risk. The butler over here shall come to the tavern every night to ensure the girl left behind is in good health and my conditions are being met. After the ball, the three of us will decide on what we do next."

Tarell frowned, thinking it over until both he and the lord accepted the conditions.

"Just one thing," said Tarell. "If at any point any of you attempt to escape, then I will consider this deal broken and I will find you, but it is not you who will be punished. If you attempt to leave this town, then as punishment the lord will be banished from it, as he is so willing to take responsibility for you. Do not forget that the lord is not the only one who carries favour in this town."

The lord nodded and agreed to his terms, and Tarell sent all three of us upstairs to decide who was to leave with me and to gather any belongings we had. As I went to head upstairs, I was stopped by my brother, who reached for my arm with a look of worry on his face.

"What are you doing?" he asked. "We can just leave. We'll be okay; I know we will. I can—"

I stopped him before he could continue. "The fact they you even came here means a lot to me. It's the first time I have felt like I have a family, but I wouldn't be much of a sister if I let you give up your life for mine. I need to do this myself."

"James," the lord said from afar, "you are more than welcome to visit my manor at any time. My Butler will give you the details, although I do ask that you do not share the information with others. And of course you are invited to the ball."

"It's okay," I reassured him. "No matter the outcome, I finally get a choice. Please don't take that from me."

He lowered his head in defeat before looking up at me with a small smile on his face. "Then you had better go pack."

Upstairs before either I or Beth could say a word, T took a deep breath and spoke in a cheery voice.

"Ah, man, I'm so jealous; I bet the lord's manor is beautiful. You will have to tell me all about it when you come back, or write me a letter after you get there. Of course I can't read, but am sure Mr Butler wouldn't mind reading it for me."

"Wait, T, what are you …" Beth began to say.

"I mean, it's out of town, right? Probably because it needs so much space. I bet there are over one hundred doors." Her voice started to crack, and a single tear fell from her eye.

"T," Beth said, desperately moving towards her.

"Please," she stated as best she could, halting Beth in her tracks, "let me do this. You have always protected me, and I could never protect you. Let me do this now; let me save you for once. Besides, in a house that big, I would feel so lost."

We both stood there, not knowing what to say or what to do.

"I'm so sorry," I said. "If it wasn't for me, this wouldn't have happened, and—"

"And nothing would have changed," T interrupted. "We would still be living in this hell with no way out. Thanks to you, we now have one. Anyway, you'd better get going."

"When you first came here, I didn't think you could last more than a few weeks, but I was wrong," Beth said, moving closer, placing her hand gently on T's cheek as tears began to fall again. "You are a lot stronger than you think and far braver than me. I won't argue with you on this, but I will promise you that in one month's time I will be back and that we are all leaving this place for good."

She pulled T in for a hug. I watched almost jealously until T pulled me in as well. I said my goodbyes to my brother, and he told me he would visit within the week. We waved bye to T as she stood at the door, a smile on her face. We kept our eyes on her until she was no longer in sight. We rode in the lord's carriage for some time silently until we reached his manor. T was right; it was indeed beautiful. But due to the long night I was unable to appreciate it fully. Instead I and Beth were shown straight to our rooms and told we would be given a tour when morning came.

The lord's Manor

10 September 1836

The manor was a sight to behold. Pure white like snow, except for a few vines attempting to reach the top, it stood taller than the trees. It was, according to the butler, about eight thousand square feet in size. Columns with a spiral pattern surrounded the manor, holding up the structure. There were three floors in total, and too many windows to count. The majority of the windows were black glass, so I couldn't see inside except through the two large ones at the front of the house, one on either side of the front door. Both of these windows were stained sapphire blue, with a mosaic image on both. One image showed a group of men killing a creature I hand never seen; the second showed the reverse. What story it was telling was a mystery, but in both pictures the creature was truly magnificent. Inside, the manor only became more enchanting.

The first thing that drew my eye was a beautiful and rather large crystal chandelier that was hanging in the middle of the entryway. It was about as big as my barn back home, if not bigger. It was about five feet across at the top, growing smaller in size going downward with each crystal. The top had individual white crystals all bunched together, forming a simple swirl pattern; after that, translucent glass of different colours shaped in sky-like patterns fell beneath it. Behind this was a large spiral staircase with a white marble banister leading all the way up to the second and third floors. Inside the manor, there was no carpet or wood; the entire building seemed to be lined with marble floors, with the occasional rug placed in some of the rooms. Just like outside, the inside was white. The marble on the floor gave a grey tone, and the ceiling was painted black, meaning there was no particular pattern. The only thing that was noticeable about it was that I could still see the odd marking from where, it appeared, it had been painted over.

To the left of the entry was a huge room that took up most of the left side of the bottom floor. This area had multiple chandeliers, though they were not as extravagant as the one in the entryway; these where on a much smaller scale. Against one of the walls was a stage with neatly arranged musical instruments on it. There were small white tables dotted around against the walls, just big enough to hold a few drinks. Next to each table hung a flower basket holding an assortment of red and white flowers. The walls were patterned with individual tees branching around the room. This was a ballroom and was going be where the lord held his ball in a month's time. It looked like it could easily entertain hundreds of guest.

To the right was the rest of the bottom floor. It started with a sitting area. There were two large brown leather couches and one black leather armchair situated in a circle, with a rug in the middle and a brown wooden table atop it. Against the walls were a few bookshelves, fully stocked, and a drinks table filled with alcohol. The only defining feature of the bare white walls was a large tapestry that hung on the right side, stretching all the way across it. Its image showed what appeared to be a family tree, but it wasn't in any language I was able to read, and the images it bore were ones I did not recognize. There were three more doors, one underneath the spiral staircase. The latter door led into a long hallway and into a large library at the back of the manor. It was filled with so many books that I doubted one could read them all in one lifetime. There was a single small armchair set in the centre with a small table next to it. One door led to the kitchen area, and another led to the garden outside. The kitchen had everything you could think of: a storage room for food, another for equipment, and a large cooking fire. In the room next to the kitchen was the dining room. The room was mostly taken up by a large antique wooden table in the centre with twenty hand-carved wooden chairs going around it. There was one prominent chair sitting at the head of the table. The walls featured trophies that must have been from the lord's successful hunts. These included everything ranging from deer to bears.

The garden was my favourite place; it felt so peaceful. The garden covered both the sides and the back of the manor. There was a small stone path that led through the garden; along the side of the path were a few small trees, but it was dominated primarily by flowers and stone sculptures. The flowers included lilies, roses, and things I had never seen before. The sculptures were of sea animals, I was told; I had never seen any before, but they all looked beautiful. Farther along the path, in the middle of the garden, situated directly behind the back of the manor, there was a single bench under a simple archway, and a small fountain in the middle. The archway was decorated with white roses, and the fountain had inside it a beautiful woman with a fish's tail .

The decor was the same throughout the manor. Upstairs there weren't as many decorations on the wall; in fact, the only decor it had was what seemed like antiques placed along the corridors on small pedestals. The ground floor was just corridors that attached to multiple rooms, all of which were locked. The ground floor was blocked by a black door that again was locked. It seemed as though we were limited as to where we could go.

My and Beth's rooms were the first two rooms one came across on the ground floor after alighting from the spiral staircase. The rooms were opposite one another, and inside they were similar. They were simply done, with a big bed in the middle, a wardrobe, and a small desk with a chair. They seemed to be the only rooms in the manor with carpet, which was a deep red and incredibly soft. The beds were covered in white sheets with black pillows. The lord's room was at the very end of the hall, and judging by the double doors leading to it, I imagined it was far more impressive than ours.

In the morning, after I and Beth had woken up, we went downstairs to find the butler and the lord preparing food in the kitchen. We joined them for breakfast, and Beth did not hesitate in asking questions.

"A manor this size … where are the other staff?" she asked.

"There are no other staff," replied the butler. "It is just me and the lord, and sometimes the odd guest—although I would call him a pest."

"But the manor—how do you possibly maintain it on your own to such a standard?" she asked.

"I don't," he said. "I and the lord both tend to the manor, and as there are only two of us, not as much work as you would think is required."

"The lord does housework?" I asked, confused.

With that the butler simply smiled, and the lord took over the conversation.

"I am not Tarell, and you are not prisoners here. All I ask is you treat us and this manor with the same respect we give you. Any of the doors in the manor that are locked are locked for a reason. Everywhere else is open to you. In the morning, you are to listen to my head butler and carry out your chores. once they are done, if there is nothing else he or I need, then you are free to do as you please."

"What about the ball?" I asked

"The ball will take place one month from now. Until then you will be helping my butler get everything ready. As for the ball itself, I will explain that closer to the time."

"I don't know why you are doing this," said Beth. "A man of your stature doesn't do anything for nothing. I don't know what it is you're planning, or why you have done this, but we want no part of it. We will do as you ask while we are here, but once the ball is over, I will be taking both Kera and T, and they will be starting new lives of their own away from this town. Until then"—she bowed—"I thank you for your generosity. We will work hard for you to show our appreciation."

The lord locked eyes with Beth and bowed his head slightly before speaking.

"A strength like yours is something to be admired; they are both very lucky to have you. I give you my word: once the month is over, whatever it is you all decide to do, it will be honoured."

We spent the remainder of the day carrying out our chores with the butler. We saw the lord on and off, but only a few times. The chores took us most of the day. We cleaned the manor thoroughly, tended to the plants in the garden, and helped prepare the food for supper. The lord did not join us; it seemed he was still busy. We had only a simple meal of potato and sausage, but it was still nicer than anything I was used to. After this we cleaned up and were told we were done for the day.

The night had begun to creep into the sky, and we were both exhausted from the long day. We headed up to our rooms, where we found fresh clean clothes on the beds for us to change into, long white gowns to sleep in, and floral dresses for the next day. The butler came to our rooms after we had changed and told us that if we wanted to write to T, he would be leaving in the hour. On the desk with the chair was an ink pot and paper. Beth joined me in my room and wrote the letter to T, explaining the events of the day. The butler returned and took the letter; he told us he would be back in the morning and ensured us that he would keep T safe in our absence. He left later that night when the moon was fully in the sky. I and Beth then said our goodnights before turning in for the night.

The Butler's Visit

10 September 1836

The night was silent, the streets empty, with small rays of light coming from the moon, illuminating the few patches they touched. As I approached the tavern near closing time for my visit, and I noticed fewer people had started to come. I assumed this was due to my lord's presence or perhaps the current lack of staff. Either way, I waited for them to close to announce my presence. Tarell saw me in and then proceeded to lock up. I asked where the girl was, and he told me she was upstairs resting. I left him to tend to the tavern as I continued upstairs. Why I expected Tarell to honour his word I do not know; perhaps it was wishful thinking. Regardless, when I entered the young girl's room, I did not like the sight that greeted me.

It looked as if I had not moved since my last visit; however, her clothes were torn, and new marks had appeared on her body. She appeared frail, as if she would break at any moment. It took her a few moments to realize who I was, but as soon as she did, it was as if she got a second breath of life. She forced a smile at me and reached out for my hand. I extended mine, and she pulled me weakly to her side. I stared at her for as few moments. The look on her face was one I was all too familiar with; she was trying desperately with a smile to hide the pain and fear behind it. She noticed the letter slightly protruding out of my pocket and asked whom it was for. I told her the letter was for her—that it was from the other girls. Her face lit up with joy. It didn't matter the state she was in; she looked as excited and happy as a small child about to receive a gift. As I handed her the letter, she simply held on to it but did not open it.

"Will you not read it?" I asked.

"Oh ... um, I will later, after you have left, sir. I don't want to be rude," she replied.

"I don't mind, miss."

"No, really, it's okay. I ... um ... have plenty of time tonight," she answered in a somewhat panicked tone.

"Miss, if I may ask, can you not read?"

She did not answer me. She put her head down almost in shame.

"If you don't mind," I asked, reaching for the letter. "Allow me."

Before reading the letter, I lay down beside her. As I did, she nestled into my chest like a small child waiting for a bedtime story. Normally I am not one for human contact, but in this instance I suppose I did not mind, and I started to read.

Dear I,

We hope everything is okay, you were right about the lord's manor; it is something to behold. We will show it to you in a month's time, as I am going to ask the lord if you can attend the ball. I and Kera have sperate rooms. The best thing about them is the beds. They are so soft and warm it feels like you are sleeping on a cloud. The house is pleasant; Kera's favourite part is the garden. It stretches around most of the house and is filled with flowers of all colours and small statues of what I have been told are sea creatures; I know you would love it. We help with work around the manor in the day, assisting the butler, who I am yet to figure out. Other than being void of human emotions, he seems loyal and trustworthy. I am glad he is watching over you. I just wanted to thank you and tell you how proud I am of you. You gave me a chance to be free of that place at your expense. No matter what happens in the time to come, remember that you are strong, brave, and kind of heart. You can do more than you think, and soon you will have your life back. If anything happens, I will be there; I won't wait for the lord's or anybody else's help. We will write again soon. Stay strong, T. And remember: no matter how dark it gets, your light alone is enough to beat anything.

We love you and we miss you.
Beth

I looked over at T. She had fallen asleep. I attempted to move, and as I did, her hand tightly gripped around my arm, and an almost worried look crept onto her face like that of a scared child begging her parents not to leave. I managed to gently get free from her grip and laid her back down onto the bedroll. She lay there, a look of despair on her face. I took this opportunity to inspect the marks on her body. It was clear they were fresh, no more than a few hours old. I removed my coat and placed it over her. As I did, she gripped it tightly like a shield, protecting her body. As I went to leave, a quiet voice whispered to me, "Thank you."

I couldn't help but be impressed by her—how she could smile as though everything was okay despite what was being done to her. In that same instant, I wondered whether it had been the same for another young girl I once knew. I went downstairs to see Tarell waiting for me. Clearly he had something to say.

"The amazing thing about that girl," he explained, "is her ability to pull anyone in. It doesn't matter who you are; her charms work on any man, and once you're hooked, it's almost impossible to let go. It can lead to the ruin of many poor men."

"Charm," I said. "What you call charm I call kindness. She may look like an easy target to others, resulting in pain and torture, but despite that she harbours no ill intent. She gives warmth to those around her, wanting nothing but for them to smile. That isn't a charm used to trick men but a strength all its own. It is far harder to forgive than it is to hate. That girl is much stronger than you know."

"Oh, it seems I have upset you. Could it be you have already fallen for her, Mr Butler?" he asked, addressing me like a child.

I walked up to Tarell, getting only a few inches from his face. The urge to simply dispose of this man here and now was extremely tempting, but I knew it would not be beneficial to my lord or the girls. I took a few seconds to calm myself before he continued.

"So how are my girls doing? Are they enjoying their temporary home and present company?"

I simply ignored his question and attempted to leave but was stopped again. It was clear he wanted information from me.

"Please don't be so rude," he sighed. "I am simply concerned for them, alone in such a big house with only the lord's company. I mean, from what I have heard, he has been alone for so long; having two women in his house, he must be having quite the time." He paused to gauge my reaction and continued to push. "I mean, after all, he is a man, is he not? Or perhaps all this time you have been satisfying his needs like a true loyal servant."

I let out a small laugh, turned to face him, and spoke freely. "It almost sounds as if you are jealous, Mr Tarell. Unfortunately, I do not think you are my lord's type. As for the two young ladies, they seem to be doing rather well. I would get used to an empty tavern if I were you."

"You're right. I would not get too attached to the girls—you or your lord. It won't be long before I have my property back," he stated confidently.

"The marks on the girl upstairs are new. How did this happen? Your instructions where not to let any harm come to her," I said politely, moving the conversation on.

"Arrrr, you see, I am here alone, and there are a lot of men who come to my tavern. I can't help it if the odd one or two customers happen to sneak past me. And what is a man to do if he sees a beautiful young lady laid out for him," he explained, grinning. "It is only natural for them to want to hold ... touch ... play."

With that, I lost my patience. I grabbed his face with my hand and pushed him back hard into the wall. As the back of his head hit the wall, he began to drop to the floor. As he did, I grabbed his arm, dangling him beneath me, keeping his knees slightly off the floor.

"'Touch,' you say ... 'Play,' you say." my grip grew tighter. I could feel his bones under my fingertips. "Tarell, do not take my lord's words so lightly—or mine." I pulled him close to me so I could whisper in his ear. "If that young girl is touched again, I will not give you the courtesy of one month; I will personally come and collect her myself and dispose of you in the process."

I released my grip, and he slumped to the floor.

"I will return again tomorrow night. And Mr Tarell, although you may have a deal with my lord, please remember that I am not just a butler and I do not take kindly to the torture of others."

With that I left and returned to the manor. The lord was waiting to hear about the girl. I lied, saying she was fine, and went to take my leave.

"Where's your coat?" he asked.

"I lost it to the wind. My apologies, my Lord."

As I began to walk inside, the lord stopped me.

"There are times when we can't help, but that doesn't mean we give up. I appreciate how hard this must be for you, given your past."

"I am fine, my Lord," I stated. "I would like to check on the other two young ladies before turning in for the night."

"Of course," he replied

Before entering the manor, I paused. "My Lord?"

"Yes."

"The ball at the end of the month—would you consider allowing I to attend? I will escort her myself."

"Do you think it wise?" he enquired.

"I think it necessary," I answered.

"Very well then. She will be your responsibility. But this is something you will need to confirm with Tarell first."

"My Lord, surely—" I started to protest before I was interrupted.

"We must approach this carefully. You know that we can't risk a repeat of what happened before. I know why you care for her so, but we must still be patient. I promise you this time will be different, but I need you to trust me. Get Tarell's approval and she may come; if not, then I am afraid there is nothing more I can do."

On that note, I checked on the girls upstairs before I turned in. They were both fast asleep. My thoughts began to wander, and I couldn't help but think, If she was still here, would she like them?

COULD THIS BE HOME?

11 TO 25 SEPTEMBER, 1836

Over the last few weeks, time here had flown by. I would normally have greeted the cold mornings with dread, but now I felt the warmth of the sun on my skin and the excitement of what each new day would bring. We had gotten accustomed to the routine of the manor. We would finish our chores by the evening, and on most days the lord would join us for meals. Although we did not see him much throughout the day, over time I felt us get closer. I became more relaxed around him. He would smile every time he saw me, and I found myself missing him daily. I didn't know whether he felt the same, but I just wanted to see him all the time, hear his sweet voice, laugh with him, and hold him close. He would always ask whether we were okay, every day, without fail. As for the butler, he would usually remain silent unless talking about T. I could see he had grown quite fond of her despite how much he tried to hide it. It was getting close to the ball, and we had yet to hear whether T could attend or not. One morning at breakfast, Beth decided to chase up the matter personally.

"How is T?" Beth asked.

"She's fine. Did you know she couldn't read?" the butler replied.

"Hmph." Beth smirked. "I knew she couldn't, but I figured you could."

"How did you know I would read it to her?"

She smiled. "I didn't; I took a chance that you would."

The butler gave a faint smile in return. "It was my pleasure."

"About the ball, my Lord," Beth said, turning to face him. "I was hoping T could join us."

"That matter has already been discussed. I believe you are speaking to Tarell about it soon?" The lord asked the butler.

"Yes, my Lord, I will be discussing the matter with Tarell soon."

"What do you mean 'discuss'?" asked Beth

"Please understand," the lord said. "T cannot simply turn up, even with me inviting her. Not without Tarell's permission."

"Permission!" Beth repeated angrily.

"If T were to leave without it, then Tarell would think she had tried to escape; he would use that as justification not just to hurt her but also to punish all of you," the lord explained. "It could result in the deal being broken, putting everyone at risk."

"But … there is no way he is going to let her go," I added.

"Yes he will," the butler said. "I give you my word."

With that the conversation fell silent.

"You had better keep it," Beth threatened.

"I always do," he replied.

We finished our breakfast in silence before carrying on. The day went by quite quickly, and before we knew it we were done for the day without chores. Beth was tired and went to her room early, but I was still wide awake, so I decided to take a walk around the manor. Before I knew it, night had come. With a black sky, a shining full moon, and a silence that covered the manor, it was so peaceful. I closed my eyes and enjoyed the feeling of tranquillity. I continued with my walk and saw a light coming from the lounge downstairs. I quietly crept towards it, tiptoeing through the halls, and poked my head around the corner to see the lord sleeping in his armchair. I couldn't help myself, and as I approached to get a closer look, before I knew it, I was face to face with him. I stood there for a few seconds and wondered to myself why a man like this would take any interest in me. The more I looked, the more entranced I became. This man was truly beautiful. Before I knew it, I had reached out my hand to caress his face, and as I did, I was stopped by the sound of his soft voice.

"If you get much closer, I will get the wrong idea," he whispered.

I immediately jumped back and apologized repeatedly. In a blind panic, I quickly turned to flee back upstairs, desperate to escape the embarrassment. But as I turned, he grabbed my arm, stopping me dead in my tracks.

"Shouldn't you be asleep?" he asked.

"I … I wasn't tired. I thought I would go for a walk," I replied, feeling my voice shaking slightly, not from fear but from excitement. The lord had a gentle but firm grip on my wrist. He began to stroke it with his fingers, and my excitement began to build. Being touched by this man sent electricity through my entire body—a sensation I had never felt before. As his fingers began to move up my wrist, I quickly snatched them away in fear he would feel my scars.

"I'm sorry … I just," I began.

"It's okay," he replied. "I apologize for touching you. It's just … you make me feel at ease." He spoke kindly, moving his arm away. "I should let you rest. Goodnight, Miss Stone."

As I began to walk away, I had to ask the question that had been weighing on my mind. "Why? Of all the people in this town, or beyond this town, why choose me?"

He smiled as he got up from his chair. Looking me in the eyes, he reached out his hand slowly, giving me time to move if I chose, and placed it gently upon my cheek. "You may not see it, Miss Stone, but you are as beautiful as you are special."

No one had ever exhibited any interest in me before, or shown me kindness, and perhaps this is why when such words were spoken to me I couldn't stop the tears falling from my eyes.

"This isn't how I used to l—" I began.

"I know how you used to look," he interrupted, "and my statement still stood true well before Tarell got his hands on you."

He wiped the tears from my face and kissed me gently on the forehead as he wrapped his arms around me. I closed my eyes and leaned into his embrace, feeling safe and loved. I didn't want him to let go. He pulled away after a few minutes, then stroked my head.

"You should sleep, Miss Stone. Perhaps in the morning we can have breakfast together, just the two of us?"

I nodded in agreement. Overwhelmed by my emotions, I found it difficult to respond. He kindly saw me to my room, giving me time to calm down a little. Before I retired for the night, I asked him one last thing.

"If it's okay … what is your name?"

"Milady, my name is Matthew," he said, bowing formally. "Please use it from now on. I never did like the title of Lord; it always sounded too presumptuous for me."

"Then please," I replied, "call me Kera."

With that I went into my room to sleep for the night. I didn't sleep for a while, as there were too many thoughts in my head—too many questions that needed answers. I tried to answer them over and over.

Why does he like me?

What does he want with me?

Does he have something planned?

Will Beth and T be okay?

Why choose now to intervene?

Does he know Tarell? Was this all planned from the very beginning?

Breakfast with the Lord

26 September 1836

Come morning I awoke happy and excited; I couldn't wait to have breakfast with the lord. I quickly got changed and attempted to make myself look as presentable as I could. Outside my room, the butler was waiting for me. Beth was already awake and downstairs. He informed me that we would all be having breakfast together this morning. I was instantly disappointed and followed him downstairs to the kitchen, where the lord was waiting. His expression was like that of a child sulking; it seemed he was as upset as I was, but he did look rather cute.

"Will you be helping us this morning?" the butler asked the lord.

"I hear Kera's skills are not great when it comes to cooking; I thought maybe I could provide some assistance," he replied, smiling.

"I still don't think it will help," Beth said, returning his smile.

With that, everyone laughed, and the atmosphere became light and friendly. The butler worked with Beth, showing her new meals, while the lord worked with me, trying to teach me the basics. I still couldn't grasp it very well. We tried over and over, but with little success, though I didn't care. Working with him, being close to him, and talking casually felt so right that I just wanted to spend the rest of my days like this. As we finished up, I thanked him using his first name. As I did, I saw his face light up.

"My Lord?" the butler said, sounding confused.

"Ah yes, well, I figured that with us all living together now, there is no need for such formalities. Besides, you know I don't like that title. I wish you would call me by my first name as well," he replied.

"You know I cannot; it would be improper of me."

"I know," he sighed. "Although that doesn't mean the rest of us have to be so formal."

"My Lord," the butler said, sounding slightly worried.

"From now on, ladies, please call me Matthew, and this here is Ray."

The butler didn't seem overly amused, but he let out a sigh and said, "If you wish."

Beth didn't hesitate. "Ray—that's an unusual name. Does it have any meaning?"

He cleared his throat. "It was a name given to me by somebody I used to know."

"Who was this somebody?" I asked

His face grew pale, and he lowered his head.

"That can be a conversation for another day," the lord said. "I will leave you to your chores, as I have matters to attend to. I need to start getting things ready for the ball."

"The ball," Beth said. "That reminds me, Ray, I was wondering if you had spoken to Tarell yet."

The butler composed himself and replied. "I will get Tarell's approval tonight."

With that we said goodbye to the lord and carried on with our day as usual.

The ball was soon approaching, so along with our usual day-to-day tasks, we began getting everything ready for it. Decorations of white silk were draped over the banisters, the flowers inside were changed to white roses, and silverware and crystal glasses were brought out of storage to use for the event. The last thing to do was pick up the food and wine the day before the event.

The butler continued with his nightly visits to T, and each time, Beth wrote to her from us both. I couldn't help but notice that every time the butler came back from his visits, he seemed a little bit happier than before he left.

In the evening, the lord gathered us all downstairs to make an announcement. He told us that an old friend of his would be visiting soon and would be staying here for a few weeks until the ball. I looked over at the butler, whose expression was one of concern. Whoever this person was, it didn't seem to be someone the butler liked or trusted.

Even the lord himself sounded hesitant; he warned us not to get too close to his guest and said that if anything were to happen, we were to come to him immediately. I looked at over at Beth, who looked as confused as I felt. We wondered who this person was who could make even the butler anxious. I didn't have to wonder for long, as we were told he would be arriving in the morning.

THE BUTLER'S VISIT

26 SEPTEMBER 1836

A dark blanket covered the sky, bringing with it the stars. The wind carried a nice chill, and the moon shone brightly. Once again Tarell had very few customers. I waited patiently for the tavern to empty before making my appearance. Tarell seemed less friendly this time; perhaps it was due to what had happened before, but either way, I counted it as a blessing that I would not have to engage with this man, so I carried on upstairs to see T. As normal, I was greeted with a heart-warming smile and took my place beside her on the bedroll. Before I read the letter to her, she asked me a question.

"I know Tarell will be going to the ball. Will I be here all alone? What if they come back?"

Fear in her eyes and voice clearly showed she was scared to death. I instantly grabbed her and embraced her tightly in a hug, and as I did, she could no longer hold back the tears and began to cry into my chest. I held her for a while, stroking her hair to try to calm her. eventually the tears stopped, and I gently used my hand to lift her chin so I could see her face. She looked up at me, her eyes red and puffy, her body shaking, and her heart pounding so hard I could feel it hitting mine. I smiled and kissed her head gently.

"That is something you don't need to worry about," I reassured her. "I will take care of it. I promise I will not leave you alone."

"I don't understand why you would do this for me."

"I made a promise to your friends that I would care for you, and I am a man who keeps his word."

She squeezed me tightly. I think she knew there was more to my reasoning than the promise I made.

"Thank you," she whispered into my chest. After a few moments, she loosened her grip and spoke once again.

"They sound happy in their letters. It won't be long before this is all over. I know you have done so much for me already, but can I ask for one more thing? When this is all over, please don't let her come back for me."

"Beth, you mean?"

"Beth was the first girl here. She has always protected me. Even in this place, she never let anyone have their way with me if she could help it, but she didn't seem to care much about what happened to herself, almost as if she had given up on her own life. When Kera arrived, it was as if she woke up; she began to fight once again, care more. And she even stood toe to toe with Tarell."

"She is indeed strong," I agreed

"You have no idea. Maybe Kera is her second chance after what happened with the other girl," she theorized.

"The other girl?"

"It's not my place to say, but both Beth and this other girl would jump into fights they couldn't possibly win. Beth wasn't always as strong as she is now; the other girl would keep her safe."

"What happened to this other girl?"

"I don't know. There are rumours, but no one knows for sure. Tarell acquired me not long after she went missing. Beth barely spoke about her, but as we grew closer, she would occasionally tell me the tales of how this girl protected her. Beth has protected me since I came here, and not once could I do anything for her. But I can now, so I am asking you, begging you—please do not let her come back. Once the ball is over, make sure the lord honours his word."

"What about you?"

"I will be okay. I will escape from here the very next day and live my own life," she said, proudly smiling, but I knew that would never happen.

"What if I rescued you?"

She buried her face deeper into my chest.

"You shouldn't joke like that."

I lifted her head once more and met her gaze with mine.

"You remind me of someone I once knew. I failed her. I wish not to repeat the mistakes of my past. You deserve your freedom as much as she deserved hers."

"Who do I remind you of?"

"She was a lot like you—small and fragile in appearance but strong in spirit. Always smiling and always wanting to make others smile. She brought kindness and warmth with her everywhere she went, as do you. I will look after you, and this time I will keep my promise."

"But the lord, Tarell, the girls and . . ." She began to panic.

"I will take care of everything. Besides, the lord could do with smiling more, and I know he would like you."

I held her for a while before reading her the letter until eventually, she fell asleep on my chest as usual. I had noticed that there were no new bruises on her, and over time the others had healed. It seemed Tarell had heeded my words.

It was only a week or two until the ball, so I headed downstairs to get Tarell's approval on I attending the ball.

"There is something we need to discuss, Tarell," I said, beginning the conversation.

"Oh, and what might that be, Mr Butler?" he snarled.

I bit my tongue before saying what came next in order to cool my temper. "I have a request for the girl."

"I thought girls weren't your type, Mr Butler. Or perhaps underneath that classy exterior there is a real man inside who wants to have some fun," he mocked.

I covered my mouth with my hand to hide the blood as I bit down on my tongue in order to restrain myself. I swallowed the blood before moving my hand away as I let out a small chuckle. "The request is not what you think."

"Then what is it? Oh, wait, let me guess. You would like Miss T to accompany you to your lord's ball. Don't look so surprised; it's obvious how much you care for that girl. Any fool could see that."

"I assume you have no issues with this, as on that night you will also be attending," I replied.

"But of course. However, if you take Miss T, then who will accompany me?" he said with a smile creeping along his face.

I knew my chances were getting lower and lower, and that if Tarell were to take her to the ball, then she would be in real danger from this beast.

"What is it you want?" I asked regretfully.

"Not much. You may come here the night before the ball and help T get ready, but you will not accompany the lord. Instead you will accompany us. You will be my servant for the night. After we have arrived and you have introduced us, she is all yours, but do not stray too far from me, as you will be keeping my glass full. You may only leave when I say you can leave," he ordered.

"I cannot just abandon the lord," I started to protest.

66

"Then I will be all alone with such a beautiful young woman, and the nights are growing colder. I know your lord will not mind. Besides, he will have two lovely young ladies of his own to entertain. I doubt he needs or even wants you there."

"And If I do this for the remainder of the ball, T is not to be touched. Also, after the ball she is to come stay at the manor with me until the fate of the girls is decided."

"You want one of my girls for the night? Were you not criticizing others not too long ago for the same thing? It will cost you, you know," he said, grinning from ear to ear.

I didn't bite back. I knew he was pushing me, seeking revenge for what I had done to him. I got what I wanted and proceeded to leave.

"There is one more small thing," he said as I reached the door. "On the night of the ball, my tavern will be empty, and people know I am a wealthy man. I would hate to be robbed. You will come here and check on the tavern for me. It won't take you too long, and you can even bring the girl if you want."

"That all?" I asked.

He walked to meet me at the door and extended his hand. "That's all, Mr Butler."

I shook his hand. It reminded me of making a deal with a devil before leaving.

"You two seem to have gotten quite close. Don't forget our agreement, Mr Butler. As you so kindly demonstrated to me, there will be consequences if you do. On the night of the ball, I will tell you when to come to the tavern. Oh, and do not mention to the lord that you will be leaving; this need not concern him."

On that note, I left.

On my return home, I gave the girls the good news about T and told the lord that Tarell had given permission for I to attend but I would need to accompany them that night. He had no issues and told me to accompany Tarell. We all turned in for the night, and my mind wandered. Tarell was up to something. Me leaving the party was not a coincidence, but why?

New Arrival

27 September 1836

In the morning, we awoke to a knock at the door. It appeared that the lord's guest had arrived. There at the door stood a young man. He didn't look much older than us. Dressed differently, he was wearing black trousers with a deep purple shirt and a loosely knotted black tie. He was quite handsome—not as attractive as the lord, but still rather appealing. His most noticeable feature was his bright red hair, the colour of fire and short, coming just past his ears, with a fringe that sat nicely just above his eyes. His eyes were blood red like ruby jewels, and when I met their gaze, it seemed as though they were shining. As he came into the manor, he walked with such confidence I could tell immediately he was comfortable in the lord's presence. I thought perhaps he was an old friend. He stood by the lord's side as Beth and I waited at the bottom of the stairs. Ray was standing close to us. The room was silent, with each person not wanting to speak or not knowing what to say, until a loud, almost childlike voice broke that silence.

"Ray, how are you? I've missed you!" the young man shouted as he waved.

We looked to the butler, surprised by how candid the guest was; and not to our surprise, Ray did not look overly impressed.

"I can happily say, young master, I have not," Ray replied.

"You're so cold, Ray. Anyway, take my bags up to my room, will you, while I catch up with—" The guest's voice was suddenly snuffed out by the lord's hand.

"I see you're as energetic as ever. How were your travels?" the lord asked.

"It went well," he said, removing the lord's hand from over his mouth. "I made some progress and found a few things out that you might be interested in."

"Another time. For now I would like you to meet my two guests," the lord said, beckoning both me and Beth to come over. Beth walked ahead of me and was the first to give her introduction. She curtseyed politely and gave her name.

"Hi, my name is Beth. It is a pleasure to meet you," she said formally.

The young man returned her formality by bowing back and giving his introduction. "Pleasure is all mine. Please call me Reno."

I then gave my introduction before he engaged us in conversation.

"Matt here did mention he had a couple of guests, but he forgot to mention that they were two beautiful young ladies. I hear there is a ball coming up; perhaps I could have the honour of taking you both with me," he said proudly.

The lord sighed like a farther disappointed in his son. I found it amusing and let out a small laugh. Beth, however, held the same expression as that of the lord—one of awkwardness.

"Okay," Reno said. "Just one then, so as not to be greedy. I heard Matt here has already snatched you up, Miss Kera, so that leaves you, Beth."

Suddenly my face turned bright red with embarrassment. I couldn't even look at the lord. What did he mean by "snatched you up"? I slyly glanced at the lord to see his expression was similar to mine.

"As much as I would love to be your second choice, I think I will attend alone," Beth told Reno as he walked up to her.

"Please don't be offended," he explained. "Out of the two of you—and no offence, Miss Stone, of course—you are far more my type. I would love to take you to the ball. Besides"—he moved closer to Beth, standing toe to toe with her at the foot of the stairs—"I think we would go together quite—"

Before he could finish his sentence, the butler appeared behind him to restrain him, but his intervention was not needed. Beth had grabbed Reno by his shirt, and with what seemed like little effort on her part, she pushed him back, making him trip over his own feet and land on his bottom. Both the lord and butler seemed delighted by this event.

"Again, I must decline your invitation. Please refrain from getting so close to me in the future," Beth said calmly. With that she grabbed me by the hand and led us upstairs. As we got to the top of the stairs, we could still hear the conversation below. We started our chores, but I made sure to linger at the top of the stairs, still able to see what was going on.

"Need a hand?" asked the butler, offering to help Reno up.

"Hmph ... where did you find someone like that?" asked Reno.

"Not your concern, but I would recommend not being so brazen with that one, Reno; she is far more capable than what you might think," said the lord, smiling.

"You're telling me. I think am in love," declared Reno. With this I saw Beth's face turn slightly red. "I have just over a week before the ball; by then she will come to like me."

"And I will have grown wings," mocked the butler.

"I didn't know you could do that, Ray. Maybe you could fly me home after the ball."

"You little ..." the butler snarled, fist clenched.

"Enough," commanded the lord. "Ray, please take his things to one of our spare rooms; we have matters to discuss. Once you have done that, come join us."

"As you wish, my Lord."

"I've missed him," Reno confessed as we heard the butler's footsteps approaching the stairs.

"I don't think his feelings for you are quite as strong. Now follow me," the lord ordered, and with that we heard a door downstairs shut and lock behind them.

Once we were upstairs, the butler advised us not to get to close to Reno. He told us that although he was harmless, he was very mischievous, and trouble seemed to follow him. We finished our chores for the day, not once seeing the lord or his guest. As night fell and we settled for bed, my brain began to torture me as normal. I had become happy here—something I didn't even know was possible. The closer we got to the ball, the greater my fear grew.

I did not want this to end. I didn't even want to leave. I had grown fond of everyone, especially the lord. I was questioning everything, and as I did, my heart quickened and my concerns grew stronger. I could feel panic take over my body like a wave crashing into me. My heart raced so much it hurt, my breath short, my body growing light as I could feel myself slipping out of consciousness where I lay. I got up from my bed and took out the blade that I had hidden. I put the cold steel against my wrist, and I could already feel my heart starting to steady. I pushed down slightly, bracing myself. Needing more pressure, I continued to push until I was ready to slice. As I did, with each cut the panic within me slowly faded away.

After I was done, I realized that one of the wounds was deeper than intended and didn't look like it was going to stop bleeding any time soon. I grabbed my wrist in an attempt to stem the bleeding, looking desperately for something to wrap around it. As I was searching, I felt a shiver crawl up my spine and detected the cold breath of someone behind me. Frozen in fear, I couldn't move as a hand was gently placed on my shoulder and a voice whispered in my ear.

"You seem hurt," said Reno.

I leapt forward, turning to see him standing in my room. His eyes, his posture—everything about him from this morning—had changed. He looked menacing, hungry even, as he walked slowly towards me, closing the gap between us. His eyes had turned brighter, and as I looked into them, a sense of calm washed over me. It was like being in a trance. My sense of fear had gone. I was relaxed and did not want to move or to flee. He reached out for my wrist and brought it close to his mouth, not once breaking his gaze. He smiled gently at me and reached into his pocket. Although I know I should have been terrified, I was not. Suddenly I felt something being wrapped around my wrist. Reno finally broke his gaze, and I could see that he had bandaged my wound. He let go of me gently, and as he did, there was a knock on the door, followed by the butler letting himself in.

"Everything okay?" the butler asked as he approached us.

"Ah, yeah. My bad, I guess I got lost again," Reno laughed as he stood in front of me to face the butler hiding my arm behind his back. "I thought this was my room. Guess I was wrong." He turned back to face me and bowed politely. "Please forgive me, Miss Stone." As he raised his head, he winked at me before leaving.

On his way out, the butler stopped him. "In the future, I would advise you to be more careful," he warned Reno.

Reno seemed to ignore his words of caution before addressing me one last time. "I would recommend finding a different night-time ritual, Kera; things like that can be dangerous—and not just for you."

With that he left. The butler remained behind to check on me and noticed the wrapping on my wrist. I could tell he knew something was up. I was certain he knew what, but he did not say anything. Instead he told me to get some rest. As he left for the door, I thanked him, and with that he stopped, and what he said next surprised me.

"We're not supposed to be alone; all living creatures desire another, whether it be for love, kinship, or kindness. Until we find that, we are never truly whole; but once we do, it is like having the sun by our sides. Everything becomes brighter, warmer, and nothing can stand against it. And like most living creatures, we need the sun to survive. Once you have yours, don't block it out by turning your back on it; use it to live."

I could tell by the tone in his voice that he was speaking from experience and had lost his own sun. After he left, I climbed back into bed. A few tears managed to escape before I eventually fell asleep.

THE LORD'S TRUE FORM

28 SEPTEMBER 1836

In the morning, we went downstairs. Reno was waiting to have breakfast with us all. He smiled at me, and I smiled back. The ball was drawing closer, and Reno had not yet given up his quest to win Beth over. For the entire day, he followed her around, attempting to engage her in conversation but very rarely succeeding, with the butler always close by. He even tried to help her with her chores and brought her flowers form the garden. Of course she accepted his help and gifts, but not his advances. By the time night had come, I could tell that she was becoming less guarded around him, engaging him for longer, and even at times starting the odd conversation with him. It reminded me of a lovesick puppy, and I thought it was adorable, letting out a small chuckle.

"It's nice to see you so relaxed," the lord said softly. "Your friend really doesn't have any fear, does she? Last night with Reno, apparently she found him later on, probably long after you had fallen asleep. She talked with him, and he mentioned that you seemed upset that night, and that he was simply checking on you. She warned him not to do anything that might cause you harm. Although I believe she was serious in her threat, it seemed to only fuel him even more in his pursuit of her.

"Wait, what?" I said, surprised.

The lord laughed. "Don't worry; he is a good guy."

"He is, but then why did the butler warn us to stay away?"

"Oh, that. Well Reno has a tendency of getting a little excitable. Last time he was here, we had to almost rebuild an entire left wing."

"*What!*" I shouted.

"Ah, you see, Reno is much like a teenager, and Ray the older serious brother, so whenever they get together, they tend to fight. You see, Reno is young and confident, so he leaps into any situation headfirst without thinking, whereas Ray, being older, is more cautious. They are the opposite of one another, but still, they do care for each other like brothers. If Reno seriously likes your friend, which I think he does, he will treat her well."

"She's seeming more relaxed around him."

"She is a perfect match for him—grounded and strong, whereas he is carefree and open. They could both do with a bit of each other. Reno is many things, but I do not entertain the company of bad people, and he is one of my closest friends."

"He does seem kind," I said, recalling the events of last night.

"He is, sometimes to his own demise."

After I and the lord had finished talking, we said our goodnights, and I headed for bed. Beth came to my room, and we talked about a lot of things. We talked about the ball, about T, and about what we would do after all of this but for each problem we had, we couldn't find a solution. It was clear that neither one of us wanted to leave and that we wanted T back. After a while, Beth began to grow tired, so I left her in my bed. Unable to sleep, I decided to take a walk outside to clear my head. As I walked through the garden, I saw the lord and Reno by the fountain. I did not see the butler anywhere, so I assumed he was still at the tavern with T. I didn't want to interrupt, so I turned to walk away until I heard a smash from behind me. Looking back, I saw Reno with his fist clenched, panting, and part of the fountain broken into pieces on the floor. I quickly hid behind the nearest bush so as not to be seen and crept close enough to hear what they were saying.

"What about us! We need you! *I* need you!" screamed Reno. "You can't run and hide forever; they will find you eventually."

"I told you we will discuss this after the ball," the lord replied calmly.

"Do you think they will last that long?"

"Reno," the lord said in a sharper tone, his expression having grown fierce. "Do not forget who you are talking to."

Reno backed away, his head low. The lord let out a loud sigh and told him to sit.

"It appears this is a conversation that cannot wait."

"You don't understand," Reno said. "We are already a dying species. There are only a few of us left. Without the first, we will become extinct. Everyone is afraid—afraid of the norms, the hunters, even each other. Most of the clans are gone. If we don't do something soon, then we *all* will be."

"We hide in plain sight; that's how we survive. It's how we have always survived since the Great War."

"It's not enough!" Reno screamed. "Someone always finds out. You can't hide who you are forever. You know that you can't always run when they find you," Reno said softly. "I'm sorry about—"

"Don't," The lord interrupted.

"Maybe if I had—" Reno began to say.

"*Enough!*" the lord shouted. His eyes had turned pure black, his face grew dark like silver, and his entire body seemed to have grown in size, his frame now resembling a bear rising to its feet. Reno slowly began to back away, terrified of the creature in front of him. As the lord crept closer to Reno, his form only grew bigger as his own clothes began to tear, until he let out a yelp of pain. An arrow had come from out of nowhere and pierced him in the back of his shoulder. In that instant, Marcus and his men came charging out of the bushes, armed with swords that I had never seen before. They looked custom made—pure silver from what I could tell—curved twice with dark black tips. I was so scared I couldn't move; I didn't know whether I was supposed to help or run. Marcus stayed back as his man pushed forward. All of them charged at the lord, and as they did, he turned to face them and let out a roar that could shake mountains, and his form changed once more, this time into something far more terrifying, completely shredding what was left of his clothes.

Wings grew from out of his back. They were as black as night, not feathered, but stretched with skin like that of a bat. His figure somehow seemed larger and stronger than before. He stood over seven feet tall, dwarfing the men in front of him. His skin had changed to a dark silver, and claws like talons had taken the place of his fingernails. His jaw was wider and deeper than it had been, as if to accommodate larger prey, and his long, sharp fangs were so big they came down to his chin, unable to fit inside his mouth. His pitch-black eyes locked with those of his assailants. As this happened, they all became frozen in fear until a voice came from behind.

"Don't be scared!" shouted Marcus, rallying his troops. "We knew what to expect; this is nothing more than a monster! Kill it now and become heroes of this town!"

As his words reached his men's ears, they let out a cry of their own and continued their charge at the lord. Three of them rushed head on, swords pointing forward. The lord brought up his arm and effortlessly swiped them away, sending all three back with such great force that they bounced off the floor. As he did so, another two came from the side in an attempt to catch him off guard. As their swords went up to strike a fatal blow, the lord's wings spread open, acting as a shield. The wings were cut deep, and the lord let out a cry of pain. As he turned, his wings knocked the men to the floor, forcing the swords out of their hands. They started to crawl away, but it was in vain, as within seconds the lord was towering over them. He grabbed one of them by the neck, easily lifting him to his level. He opened his mouth wide and brought the man closer to take a bite out of his neck. As his teeth where inches from the man's throat, the other one grabbed his sword once more and lunged for the lord's chest. With his other hand, the lord grabbed the second man. Holding them both high up by their throats, he resumed his meal until a large net was thrown over him, interrupting him once more. In an attempt to break free, he released the two men. As he struggled, the remaining force started to circle him.

"Now, while he is trapped, ki—" Marcus began to shout, but all of a sudden he had stopped.

Seemingly confused, the men looked behind them for further orders. Marcus was simply standing still in what seemed like a trance, and instantly I recognized it. It was the same trance I had been in with Reno that night. I looked around, and as I had guessed, I saw Reno from a distance, staring at Marcus. It looked as if he was whispering something, and as he did, Marcus began to talk.

"Put your weapons down," Marcus instructed his men.

"*What?* Are you serious! Look at this thing! We need to—" The man who was speaking also stopped, but not because of Reno. The lord was no longer under the net; the only thing I could see in his eyes now was bloodlust. He let out a blood-curdling roar and began to lunge from man to man. The first man he tore in half; he slit the throat of the second. The other one was bitten so hard his head was torn almost completely off. In what felt like only seconds, he had decimated the men, leaving only Marcus.

Blood covered the floor and the lord. His gaze snapped to Marcus as he began to slowly approach. Marcus, still stuck in Reno's gaze, was unable to move. As the lord grew closer, he let out a deep growl. Closer and closer he got. My heart beating faster, I couldn't bear to see any more killing. When the lord was only a few feet away, I leapt out of the bushes and screamed for him to stop. As I did, like a startled animal he raised his hand to strike me down. Reno dashed desperately towards us, releasing Marcus from his trance. I closed my eyes hard and raised my arms as a shield. Knowing it would do very little, I braced for death.

Nothing happened. At first I thought the strike was so clean that I had instantly died on the spot, until I peeked out of one of my eyes and saw Ray standing in front of me. One arm was behind his back, and the other had grabbed the lord's wrist, stopping him dead in his tracks. Holding the lord securely in place with what seemed like little effort for him, he turned to me and asked that I back away. I couldn't believe what had happened, and I certainly could not move. Reno had appeared by my side and guided me back to a safer distance.

"My apologies for being late, my Lord; it seems like a missed quite a lot," Ray said. "You need to calm down and return to your other from. You are scaring Miss Stone."

The lord glanced over to me, and his eyes began to change back to normal. As they did, I could see the pain behind them. His body began to shift back, but it seemed like one of the men was not quite dead. With his final breath, he sprang up from the floor and let out a desperate cry as he lunged at the lord with his sword. Ray immediately released his grip in an attempt to stop the attack, but as the lord turned to face the man, he turned into the sword slicing at his side. He let out a defining scream, then lunged his hand forward, piercing straight through the man's chest to the other side, leaving his heart firmly in his grasp. He paused for a moment before squishing the heart like a tomato in his grip and pulling his arm back out of the man. He let out a feral roar far louder and far more terrifying than before.

"It appears you can no longer hear me, can you; I apologize for my actions, my Lord," Ray said sincerely before he arched his back and lowered himself like a big cat ready to pounce.

As he looked up at the lord, I saw that his eyes had also changed, but they were not black; instead they were golden yellow. He had no teeth, wings, or fangs, but just bright yellow eyes. He lunged towards the lord, and after that it was hard to keep up with his movements. He wasn't just fast; he was so fast that it looked as though he had vanished from one spot to another, just like magic. Instantly he was behind the lord. He moved around him easily, dodging any attack the lord threw at him, over and over. The lord grew more and more infuriated until he spread his wings out wide and stomped hard on the ground, splitting the earth beneath him. As he did, Ray leaped high into the air. As he came back down, he landed on the lord's back. Using the momentum of his jump, he pulled the lord back hard, smashing him into the floor. Knocked down, Ray quickly pulled out a small vial from around his neck that appeared to be on a chain. He opened it up and placed it under the lord's nose like smelling salts. He kept the lord pinned as best he could, but not without taking a slash from one of his claws. Not even flinching, Ray kept the lord locked until he began to stop struggling. His body became relaxed, and as it did, his form started to change back. Ray removed himself from the lord and walked over to Reno and me. He took Reno's coat and walked back to the lord, covering him up. He then looked over to the both of us.

"Reno, if you could kindly escort Miss Stone to her room, I will be there shortly to attend to any injuries," he stated politely.

"Of course," Reno replied.

"Oh, and once you have done that, you might want to go tie up any loose ends. When you come back, we will need to talk," Ray said in a more intimidating tone.

I could feel Reno's hand on my shoulder; it was trembling slightly. This confident, seemingly fearless man was now afraid of what was to come. He took me back to my room, and as he went to leave, Beth came out of hers. As he saw her, he looked almost ashamed and hid his face as he made a hasty retreat. Beth saw me and quickly pulled me in for a hug; she had seen everything from her room, and I could hear her heart pounding out of her chest.

"We need to leave now!" she said, trying to drag me into her room. I planted me feet firmly and stopped. "What are you doing? This might be the only time we can leave. We will get T, and the three of us can leave this town."

"No," I stated.

"*What?*" she snapped back "And why not?"

"Because he looked like he was in pain."

"Who?"

"The lord."

We both stood there in silence for a while, trying to come to terms with everything that had just happened until she tried to convince me again to leave once again.

"You saw what I did, right? What he did to those men ... what if that was you, or me, or ..."

"He won't!" I snapped at her. "Those men—they attacked him first; they hurt him first. I know what he did was wrong, but he did it to protect himself. Since the beginning, he has been nothing but kind to me—to both of us. I won't turn my back on him now."

"He isn't even human. I don't even know what he is," she said desperately.

"Just because he is different, that doesn't make him a monster."

Beth let out a heavy sigh. "You're really not going to leave are you?"

"No," I answered.

"I guess we'll be here for a bit longer than Ray," she said.

As I turned around, I saw the Butler behind me, his arm bandaged.

"It would appear so. Miss Stone, the lord has requested your presence back outside—only if you want to, of course. He would like a chance to explain himself. Beth, Reno will be back shortly. I am sure you have questions. I think it best he answer them, as I must be off. There is something I need to attend to urgently. But I will be back before sunrise."

"Ray," Beth said calmly, "as of this moment we entrust our lives to you and the lord. You don't need to tell us not to say anything; however, if harm comes to Kera or T, it doesn't matter what you are; you will regret it."

"Out of all of the threats I have had over my time, Beth, yours is one I take very seriously, and I have no doubt that I would indeed regret it. I promise you none of you will come to harm," he said respectfully.

"Very well. When Reno returns, tell him I will be waiting for him in my room." As she said this, she turned to go back to her quarters. "Kera, I appreciate what you said, and I will keep it in mind, but remember that some people in this world are nothing more than what they appear to be."

Ray took me back outside, where the lord sat waiting patiently by the broken fountain. As Ray took his leave, he bowed politely. I walked over to the lord, and before he could say anything, I asked him whether he was okay. With that, a single tear fell from his eye and he let out what seemed to be a sigh of relief as his posture suddenly relaxed, and I sat down beside him.

"After everything you saw, everything that happened, that's what you say to me?" he said, letting out a nervous laugh.

"To be honest, I don't really know what happened, but I do know that you got hurt."

"I am okay; I heal quickly."

"Reno seemed quite upset. I hope he's okay as well," I said, staring at the sky.

"You are truly remarkable," he said, his hand reaching for my cheek, turning my face to his. "Of all the thousand responses you could have given, the many things you could have done, your first concern is ensure we are okay." He smiled.

"You got hurt. Reno seemed sad. It is only natural to make sure your friends are okay."

With that he pulled me in and hugged me tightly. I could feel another tear fall from his eye down my cheek. I hugged him back, and for a while we stayed like that, until he gently released me.

"Most people, Miss Stone, run from monsters."

"I am not most people," I answered. "Besides, you may have looked scary, but that doesn't make you a monster. I don't think anyone is born a monster, or cruel. People are shaped that way over time because of the things they do and what is done to them. These people come in all shapes and sizes, and it is their actions that make them who they are, not what they look like. You have shown me and my friends nothing but kindness. how could that possibly make you a monster."

"Others would disagree."

"Others are wrong! Although I am curious as to what you are?"

"Then I will do my best to explain."

By that time, Reno had returned. His clothes were scuffed, and there was blood marks on his collar.

"My Lord … am … I didn't mean …" he started to say.

"It's okay, Reno; I know why you said what you said, and you weren't entirely wrong, I promise after the ball we will discuss this further, and we will do something to help them. You have my word."

"Reno, Beth is waiting for you in her room," I said politely

"I think it best if I didn't—"

"I would suggest you go," I interrupted. "She can be far more intimidating than you think, and besides, she isn't one to judge."

"Thank you," Reno said, and he took his leave to go see Beth. I could tell he was nervous.

A VAMPIRE

"Well, Kera, let me do my best to explain what we are and how we came to be. We still don't know who was first, us or the humans. All we do know is that we are mutations of each other. Did we mutate from humans and evolve into what we are, or did humans mutate from us? As our design is very similar, it's hard to know for sure.

"Your kind eat, drink, and sleep to survive. You reproduce with a mate, and this is cycled throughout the generations. We are no different, but our process is unlike that of humans. We don't need food or water to survive. We can consume them, but we gain nothing from it. The body treats them as foreign substances and simply disposes of them by destroying them from the inside. In some cases, this can cause ill effects, so we try to avoid it altogether. Our bodies run on blood instead. In humans, blood runs through the entire body, carrying things like oxygen that you need to breathe. We are similar. We, too, require blood, but not oxygen. However, the way our bodies function is different. Our mutation changed our hearts; they became smaller and far more complex. We call it the master cell; it is what you would call a heart. It doesn't have a time frame like yours, and it will last as long as it is cared for, meaning my kind are immortal. The cell is layers upon layers of tissue, muscles, and nerves. It is connected to everything inside the body; like the heart, it pumps blood throughout. The body has changed to run off this one master cell, which is powered purely by blood. The master cell constantly supplies blood at an incredible rate through the entire body, thousands of times quicker than that of a human, allowing for regeneration and increased speed, strength, vison, and more. Every sense, every part of the body, is enhanced immensely. It is also the reason why we don't need to sleep; we run purely off blood; so long as we have it in our bodies, we have no need for rest."

"I don't understand. If you are this, strong why aren't you ruling over all humankind? Why were those men able to hurt you?" I asked.

"We cannot produce our own blood. Call it an evolutionary flaw. That means we are only as strong as the amount we can consume. Although we can run off a small amount, it makes us very weak—almost human-like, if not weaker. With only a small amount, the blood can only do the bare minimum of keeping us alive, making us vulnerable. As I mentioned before, we are not that different from you. We can be killed; it's just very hard to do so. The master cell is what keeps us alive, so it is encased in bone far stronger than yours. It's almost impossible to pierce unless by another one of our kind. Those swords from earlier—the black tip on the end is bone from my species; our bone is black."

"How did they get those?"

"I don't know, but it concerns me that they did. Just like you, Miss Stone, we have hearts. They may look and act differently, but they are still the same. And like you, without a heart we cannot live."

"What about decapitation?" I asked brazenly.

The lord laughed. "Honestly, that I do not know and do not want to find out. There have been tales in the past of my kind dying to it, and others say their heads simply regrow. We are not sure if the master cell can survive without the brain or if it even can be regenerated. Other body parts can, such as limbs. A cut on your finger would take a few days to heal; for us it would heal immediately. A lost limb could not be replaced for you, but for us it would take days, maybe a week.

"Long ago, people began to figure out what we were; and because of that, other creatures that aren't exactly human were also brought to light. Because of the way we looked, we were immediately seen as a threat and hunted by humans known by us as the secundos."

"Wait. Other creatures? You mean there are others out there different from you?"

"This world is very large. It is filled with all kinds of creatures. It just so happens that over time your species grew quicker than any other, dominating the majority of the lands, leaving the rest of us to hide away, as you don't take kindly to those who are different to you. Over time, specialized weapons were made to combat our power and give the humans a fighting chance. Both sides turned on their own kind as well; there were those who sided with the humans, and humans who sided with us. It continued for hundreds of years until eventually the great war broke out. Creatures from all over came together to kill humankind once and for all; they felt it was in their right to take back what humans had so greedily taken from them. The war lasted almost a decade, and in that time the body count was colossal. A lot of creatures on our side were the last of their kind and in the Great War became extinct. As the war raged on and casualties rose on both sides, there was no clear winning side, so men and creatures on both sides met in secret to find a way to stop the war. They feared that if it continued, both living things and the earth itself would be consumed. They were successful, but our numbers had dropped drastically. We decided to hide away in the shadows so we could recover. Over time, as we regained our strength, some were too afraid to come back out, whereas your kind continued to grow."

"Can a human become a vampire?"

"Maybe, but it is forbidden to do so. After the war, we needed a council to watch over and monitor creatures from all over the world. So one was formed, with a representative from each region and as many races as were left. It was decided that no unnatural creatures would ever be made.

"Some of us are able to share our essence through things like bites. This is then transferred to the host—in this case, a human. When this happens and is accepted by the host, our essence combines itself with the human and takes over, replacing the human parts inside and turning the person into a vampire. In some cases, although very rare, this is a complete success and all traits of the human form are gone and the individual becomes what he or she was bitten by. In other cases, our essence isn't able to fully take over, so it bonds together, making the individual have both vampire and human parts. This creates a hybrid. There are very few of these, and not all are half vampires and remain somewhat of a mystery."

"What happens if they don't turn or become a hybrid?"

"They die. The human body sees our essence as a threat and, instead of accepting or bonding with us, tries to eliminate it. This causes a chain reaction throughout the host, killing of all the cells one by one until nothing remains; it is an unpleasant sight and the reason why it is forbidden. Our mutation is natural; to force that onto another living thing is not, and it is why almost all the time the individual dies or, worse, becomes unrecognizable."

"Unrecognizable?"

"It doesn't matter; there are those of us who can reproduce normally with another mate of our kind. In fact, that is the case for all of us, as far as I know."

"Does this mean you can?"

"Yes. As I said, we are not that much different to you; our bodies run and function similarly to yours, and we, too, can have children. They grow up just like your kind; the master cells start off small and grow stronger over time. The only difference is that in our species, men's bodies have adapted to also be able to carry children. Both males and females can fertilize one another and carry children."

"What! How would that even—"

"I would rather not go into it."

"Okay. If I can continue to pry, what about Reno? When he looked at Marcus earlier and when he looked at me, it was like being in a trance."

"As I said, our bodies are similar to yours but not the same. In Reno's case, his eyes are able to entrance others and make a telepathic connection, meaning he can implant thoughts into their heads, kind of like mind control. Some vampires have these traits, and some don't. It is mainly the half breeds that have these abilities; our kind believe it is caused by having both human and vampire essence."

"And what about you? I mean, what you changed into—is that one of these abilities?"

"I am much older than Reno, and there are only a few like me. We are known as the firstborns, the first of our kind, and are much stronger. Unlike in the case of the human heart, where time is your enemy, chipping away at your life, for us time is our ally. The longer we live, the stronger our master cell gets. We firstborns are believed to be the first of our kind; we have lived for thousands of years, making us incredibly strong. We also have the ability to transform into what you may see as batlike creatures. This was never passed on to any of our young, meaning only we can do this. We are not sure why. The theory is that our bodies decided it was an unnecessary feature and did not pass it on to the next generation, but no one is certain. It is not an ability like the one Reno has but is simply something our bodies can do. Each firstborn's form is different, but they all work the same."

"You say that it's mainly half-breeds who have abilities; does that mean Reno?"

"It is not my place to tell you his story."

There was a moment of silence. I could tell Reno was a sensitive topic, and I didn't want to push, so I moved on.

"Wow. Different creatures, wars no one knows about ... the world really is a big place."

"There is so much more you do not know, but for now I think that will do. I will personally go pick up T and escort the three of you out of town. I have a home you can use. I will provide money, of course, and ..."

"You know, when I came here, you told me you weren't like Tarell or the others and that I had a choice, so why are you now trying to take that away?"

"I assumed that—"

"You assumed wrong. I have no intention of leaving. We have a ball to attend, do we not? Although I have nothing to wear."

"Then I had better get you something."

After that, we went back to the house and saw Beth and Reno downstairs. Reno seemed happy, so I assumed all had gone well with their talk. We finally called it a night, knowing the next weeks or so we would be busy with the preparation for the ball.

Morning of the Ball

10 October 1836

There was not much to write about over the days that followed. Up until the ball, it was routine. We were all busy playing our parts in getting everything ready, and before we knew it, the day had come around. That day, however, would be one of the longest days in my life. That night seemed colder than usual, and as I looked up into the night sky, I couldn't help but wonder whether things could have turned out differently. It all started the morning of the ball.

The lord, Reno, and the Butler were all waiting downstairs for us. They had decided to take us to town so we could choose dresses for tonight, as well as jewellery, make-up, and even perfume. Excited, we hastily got changed into elegant casual dresses the lord had provided for us and went downstairs. Reno was wearing his purple waistcoat with white vest and black trousers; the butler was wearing the same but with a black waistcoat. The lord was in all black, with a long trench coat that reached to the floor. We got into the carriage and headed to the town. On the way, I realized that I had never once seen the lord in town or even in the sun.

"Can your kind go outside during the day?" I asked curiously.

"Hmph. Yes, but it fatigues us," the lord replied. "As I mentioned, our bodies run on a lot of blood and at a very quick pace. You can regulate your body temperature to stay warm during the winter, but we have no need for this. Our skin is far tougher and more durable than yours, so the cold and the heat don't really affect us. This means our bodies are almost always cold, as they don't need warming up. This saves more energy to be used for other things. However, it has its disadvantages. Direct contact with sunlight seems to slow down our bodies' functions. The sun's rays trick the body into thinking it needs to cool down, meaning the whole time we are exposed, our bodies are working overtime to stay cool, using up a lot of our energy. If we are left exposed for a long time, it can put us into a hibernation state, not killing us but getting us as close to death as can be."

"How would you fix that?" I asked

"You can't. The only way is to have someone else fix it for you by taking you out of the sun and replenishing the blood."

"It is a method sometimes used as punishment," Reno added.

"Punishment for what?" I replied.

"Nothing. Let's talk about kinder things, shall we," the lord insisted.

"Sun. Hmph. Nice to know," Beth said

"Why is that nice to know?" Reno asked, sounding concerned. "Beth? *Beth!*"

With that, we couldn't help but laugh. The conversation changed to Reno telling us about his travels, how he got here, the various towns he had visited, and the landscapes he had crossed. It sounded truly amazing. Before we knew it, we had arrived in the town. On our entry, people's eyes were all over the carriage. Other than the time the lord came to my aid, I don't think he had ever entered the town before. As we approached our first destination in the wealthier part of town, my stomach began to knot as I dreaded opening the carriage doors. I took a deep breath and felt the lord's hand in mine. He squeezed it tightly and smiled. Beth had done the same with Reno, to his surprise. We looked at each other, took deep breaths, and stepped outside.

As we stepped out of the carriage and into the light of day, it was almost as if the entire town froze; everyone had stopped in the track to stare. Whispers filled the air. Some people didn't even recognize us, whereas others couldn't believe it was us. As if on show, we walked to the dress store, only to be blocked by three familiar faces. It was Charlotte and her friends.

"So this is what sleeping with the lord gets you!" she shouted for whole town to hear. Chuckling, she continued. "I see you were so ugly that Tarell had to fix you just so you could service men. Then you went and served the lord so you could steal his riches. We were right about you, nothing but an evil—"

"And what are you!" I shouted, my hand desperately clutching the lord's as I could feel him clutching back. "A personality so twisted and vile that she has only her looks to cling to—something that will soon run out."

"How dare you, you little—!" Charlotte shouted, raising her hand to slap me. As she brought it down to strike, it was grabbed by Beth. With ease she pushed Charlotte back so hard she fell to the ground.

The entire town gasped. I took a second and looked at the people beside me. I realized in that moment that I had all the strength and support I needed to no longer hide, no longer be afraid of who I was or of anyone else—to stand up for myself and, for the first time in my life, fight back. I no longer needed to be ashamed of who I was, because I was enough—enough for me to be loved, respected, cared for, and treated as an equal.

"My whole life, everyone has thought nothing of me—expected me to be nothing, to do nothing—so I always thought I was nothing: no one worth saving, no one worth being here, sitting alone in the bottom of the deepest, darkest well, looking up, praying for a hand to pull me out, knowing it would never come. I felt I was stuck forever, unable to climb out, waiting for death to take me." I paused, my body shaking. I looked at Beth, the lord, Ray, and Reno. I firmly planted me feet into the ground, took another breath, and, for the first time in my life, spoke my mind. "It wasn't just one hand that pulled me out of that dark place; it was a number of them. They reached out and pulled me out of my misery and showed me what life is suppose to be. I'm happy, not because of riches or looks but am happy with who I am, with the company I keep and the life I get to choose. My days from now on will bring me only joy, whereas yours will be filled with disappointment. I'm not the monster or the ugly one, Charlotte; you are."

The entire town remained silent. No one moved, every person hanging on my words with a look of disbelief. I walked towards Charlotte, no longer afraid.

"I had forgotten how precious life is. It is a gift for everyone to enjoy in his or her own way. The ability to make one's own choices is something that shouldn't be taken away or controlled, and mine never will be again."

I offered Charlotte a hand up. Still in shock, she simply sat there until whispers once again filled the air. She slapped my hand away and pulled herself to her feet.

"You think some kind of a makeover or fancy clothes make you or her any different. Inside you are still both the same: ugly, horrid whores."

"Miss Charlotte, is it?" the lord said, stepping between us, Reno by his side. They both stood intimidatingly in front of her. it seemed that they did not like hearing what she had to say, and I could see they were both struggling to remain calm. "Miss Stone has said her piece, and I believe so have you. I would advise you to leave and not bother her or Beth again, otherwise I may have to speak with your farther directly. Remember where his money comes from and just how quickly it can be taken away."

"Or," Reno suggested, his eyes glowing red, "we could always go somewhere a bit more private and settle this amongst ourselves."

The colour from Charlotte's face had drained to pure white. She looked paler than I. Shaken, she quickly scampered to her feet and walked away in a rage. Knowing Charlotte, I was aware that this wasn't over. I knew I would see her again. As the lord looked up at the town, he sent an almost universal message. The onlookers lowered their heads, the whispers stopped, and people carried on about their days.

"I am so proud of you," Beth said, putting her arm around me. "I knew you had it in you."

"it helps when you're not alone."

Beth smiled and hugged me tight, and we continued into the shop. The shopkeepers had witnessed what had happened outside and were clearly nervous. There were only a few dresses, but they were all handmade, so elegant and beautiful, made to the finest standards of quality. We didn't know what to choose, and the lord recommended we try some on while he and Reno rested.

I could see the sun had taken its effect on the lord, but Reno didn't seem as worse off. We tried dress after dress until we settled on the ones we liked. We both chose silk. Beth's was a deep purple so as to match Reno, although she swore that wasn't the case. It was slim fitting, with only a single purple rose on the shoulder and went down to her ankles. Mine was pure black to match the lord's, which was intentional;

it hung off the shoulder with a small dip across the chest. It fitted my body perfectly, showing my figure. There was a slit in the leg on the left side that started at my upper thigh. The dress went down to the floor, stopping an inch off it. Both the lord and Reno were lost for words.

We finished our shopping, and the lord and Reno picked out jewellery that matched our dresses as gifts for us to wear, and finally we picked up the perfume. Once done, we headed back to the manor. Reno seemed to only just start looking a bit tired, but the lord seemed about to collapse.

Back at the manor, there was a line of staff waiting outside. Ray had recruited help for the night. He told us to go inside and relax until the ball tonight, stating that he would get everything ready and bring T by later once the ball had started.

"Oh no!" I cried. "We didn't get T a dress."

"Don't worry; I already have one picked out for her. Now please go rest."

We entered the manor, and I could see that the lord was struggling. I told Beth I was going to take him to his room, and Reno quickly said he also needed to rest and looked at Beth. She simply rolled her eyes and began to walk towards the garden, Reno giving chase behind her. I took the lord upstairs to his room and helped him onto the bed. As I moved to leave, he grabbed my hand.

"You were amazing today," he complimented me.

"I couldn't have done it without Beth, without you," I replied shyly.

"I don't think that's true; I think you had it in you all along. We just gave you a little nudge."

"I hope you will always be there to nudge me when I need it."

The lord sat up and gently pulled me down to the bed. He turned to face me and ran his hand over my neck.

"If you need it," I offered, placing my hand over his.

"I could manage, but in all honesty, I don't want to; I would much rather devour you instead."

With that, he gracefully twisted my body and placed me gently onto his bed, his form over mine, his body inches from touching mine, hovering above me.

"Are you not scared—not even a little?" he asked.

"Right now, yes, but for a whole other reason," I replied trembling not with fear but with excitement. My entire body was filled with what felt like electricity.

"I won't let you go; I won't let you leave once I have you," he whispered as his face grew closer to mine.

"Then it's a good job I don't want to go," I whispered back.

He looked me deep in my eyes. "I promise I will protect you," he said, leaning his forehead against mine and closing his eyes. As he did, I closed mine and responded softly.

"And I you."

I suddenly felt the sharpness of his fangs as they pierced the skin on my neck, it was only a brief moment of pain followed by a rush of excitement. I could feel him sucking harder and harder, closing the gap between our bodies as blood began to trickle down my neck and onto my breasts.

As he finally released his grip, I opened my eyes and was met with a kiss—my first real kiss—and it was like an explosion through my body. I felt myself almost come to life. My temperature rose quickly, my heart quickened, and the electricity intensified, and before I knew it my arms were around his neck, pulling him in tight. The only thing I could feel was him, and I wanted to feel more.

I kissed him back hard. As I did, I felt his body press up against mine. His hands moved slowly; one firmly grasped my hair, and the other moved down, forcibly moving my legs apart. He then started to trail his fingers along my inner thigh, slowly reaching up. The closer he got, the more excited I became. I could feel the anticipation building inside of me. He ran his hand softly up and down my thigh almost as though he was teasing me.

"Please," I begged. "Touch me."

"I am. Tell me where."

His hand was now inches from my private area. I begged again, "Touch me."

"Where?" he whispered, kissing me neck.

"My private area."

"You mean here?" he flipped me over and bit down hard on my bum. I let out a moan of pleasure. He began softly kissing it from cheek to cheek as I felt my dress start to tear.

"No … I mean …" I was barely able to speak; the pleasure was so intense I didn't care what he did to me.

"Then try again," he playfully stated.

"Please … touch me … touch my vagina."

"Good girl." He grinned.

With that he pulled me up by my hips so I was on all fours, and he ripped of what was left of my dress, leaving me exposed on his bed. He licked his fingers and then plunged them hard inside of me. The feeling was incredible. He plunged over and over, thrusting them hard. He grabbed me by my hair, pulling my head back as my body moved forward. Over and over, I could feel something building up until he stopped. I slumped down, already tired. I could feel myself dripping wet. He took his time, what felt like hours, simply toying with my body.

"Don't tell me you're tired," he said as he began to strip. "We still have all day before the ball."

He finished removing all of his clothes, then reached out for the torn dress, using part of its shreds to cover my eyes. As I was without the ability to see, my body became far more sensitive. I could feel a cold breeze sweeping over my naked body, gently nipping at my breasts like small teeth taking a bite. The next thing I felt was the cold of metal on my wrists. I couldn't see what it was, but I could tell I was being restrained.

"What an enchanting sight," he said erotically.

My arms were bound to the bed; only my legs had movement.

"Now then, shall we begin?" he asked, taking what sounded like a sip of a drink.

He came back over, and I felt him climb onto my body, mounting me. He kissed me, gently at first, then more intensely. I could taste the bitterness of the wine as his kisses grew fiercer. He eventually released my lips, and I let out a gasp for air. I knew it must have been at least an hour by now, if not longer. I could feel my body growing weaker. I didn't know how much longer I could stay in this state of anticipation.

I felt him climb off me, and I heard the striking of a match. I didn't know what he was planning, and a slight terror ran down my spine.

"Don't worry; not all pain is bad pain."

With that I felt something hot fall onto my belly. At first the shock made me flinch. He did whatever he was doing again. This time I didn't flinch; instead it made me hotter. The strange heat was intense, not so hot at to burn me, but just enough to stimulate me. The sharpness of the heat focused on one spot, directing all of my attention to it. He did it again, this time further up; I could feel the intense heat driving my body mad. He dripped it again, this time directly on my nipple. I let out another moan of pleasure; it felt truly amazing. He did it again on the other breast, and again I moaned. My breathing had got faster. There was so much build-up going on inside of me that I was struggling to even know where I was, lost completely in the moment.

He walked around me, torturing my entire body like this over and over for what felt like an eternity. I didn't know whether I would pass out or simply go mad from the pleasure before he was done with me. He began to drip the wax back to my stomach and down towards my vagina. I took a deep breath, excitedly expecting the next one to fall between my legs, anticipating the same sensation. Instead I felt the cold of his fingers enter deep inside me. The contrast from hot to cold sent a shock through my entire body. Parts of me were still warm where the heat had hit, and yet something cold was inside me. I could tell it was his fingers as they massaged inside, touching my innermost parts. He thrust them hard, over and over, this time quicker, moving my entire body with each thrust. Again I felt a build-up, and I moaned loudly until once more he stopped just before I climaxed. I took a deep breath, wondering how much more of this I could take.

"Please … I don't know how much longer …" I begged desperately.

"How much longer what?" he replied.

"How … much longer … I can last," I panted, still breathing heavily.

"Don't worry," he assured me. "There are still a few hours of daylight left that we can use before the ball."

"What … but … the day …" I said, confused.

"Hmmmmm, we haven't used all of it yet. We still have some light left in the day if you can manage it."

I took a deep breath, not knowing what would come next. I could feel his breath on my thighs. Then I felt his tongue moving slowly up. Further it went, until it reached my vagina. Slowly and softly, he began to massage my clitoris. The feeling was different from anything I had felt before. Every time he did something new, it gave a different sense of pleasure, all building into one. My legs instinctively tried wrapping around his neck, but with both hands he forced them down, pinning them into position, and the sensation built. I was getting close again. *Just a bit more and …*

He stopped once more.

"Please," I begged "… please let me finish."

"Perhaps we should stop; I wouldn't want you tired for the ball tonight."

"Please, no more teasing, no more fingers."

"Oh, then what do you want,"

"You."

"Me?"

"You … I need your cock inside me … now … please … I am begging you."

"Then how can I say no."

He untied the chains, ripped off my blindfold, and flipped over onto all fours. I felt him come behind me. Slowly he placed his cock against my vagina, and with one thrust he was in. This was very different to his fingers—and far more pleasurable. Once he was inside of me, one of his hands firmly gripped my waist while the other grabbed a handful of hair. He started to move slowly at first, then soon enough the pace quickened, and the force with which he was thrusting became stronger. As it did, my moans grew louder and louder. That feeling had come back and was building once again. Over and over he pounded deep inside me. I could hear his moans, making it more exciting. He leant down and bit hard into my neck, drawing blood yet again and hitting me with an intense shock of pleasure.

The faster he got, the stronger the feeling became. Suddenly he spun me hard onto my back. I could see his face; his look was mesmerizing, like that of a predator devouring its prey. I was locked into his gaze, and he lifted my legs up high and plunged hard into me once again, deeper than before. My hands reached up to grab something so I could brace myself, but before they could he grabbed both of my wrists with one hand, securing them above my head, as the other slowly moved down to my throat, gently squeezing. His pace had quickened once more, and I could feel myself almost at climax once again. As I came closer and closer, his grip around my throat tightened. Harder and harder he squeezed; faster and faster he got. The feeling was building, climbing to its maximum. He squeezed once more, almost cutting off my air completely. One last time he thrust deep, and I could feel the warmth of him flow into me, filling me up inside as my body exploded with pleasure.

He kept hold of me for a few minutes as more and more of him was released into me. My body relaxed as it became weak. As he finished, he released his grip and moved to lie beside me. With what little strength I had, I climbed onto his chest, wrapped my leg over him, and nestled in. I looked up to see him smiling before I could no longer stay awake.

The Butler's Visit

10 October 1836

More excited than usual, I found myself arriving at Tarell's tavern sooner than I expected. It was the night of the ball. I arrived and let myself in, but something was strange; the lights were all out, and the Tavern was silent. I instantly rushed upstairs to T's room, but she was not there, I searched Tarell's but still found nothing. To my horror, I spotted blood on the floor. As I followed the trail, it took me towards the cellar downstairs. When I entered, the sight that greeted me sent shivers to my very soul; wrists bound by rope, ankles tied together, there was a small girl dangling from a hook in the ceiling in the middle of the room with blood dripping down off of her and onto the floor. Painted almost red by it, she looked like fresh meat not long butchered. I could tell immediately it was T, and from behind crawled out Tarell with a smile on his face and his hands stained red.

"I have a friend," he said, "Who's rather knowledgeable in the human body, especially a woman's, so he helped me prepare her for you."

My entire body filled with rage, and in an instant, I dashed across the room and held Tarell up by his throat, slowly squeezing the life from him.

He laughed, gasping for air. "So you are not human either, I see." I tightened my grip. "If you don't want her to die," he said, still desperately gasping for air, "I would let go. That friend I told you about also happens to be rather good with poisons."

Reluctantly I released my grip, dropping Tarell to the floor, and headed towards T. I took her down slowly and placed her onto the floor. I removed my shirt to cover her up and checked for any serious injuries. Luckily there were none; instead she had multiple gashes. Fortunately they were not deep enough to keep bleeding, but there were so many all over her body that the blood loss was still serious; this had been done carefully.

"I wasn't sure about you," Tarell said as he started to rise to his feet. "Now I know."

"What do you want?" I asked.

"The same thing everyone wants—power. The same power, it seems, you and the lord have. I have been watching him for years, patiently waiting. I knew his visits into town were not without purpose. I had almost given up hope until that day. You never stopped for anything until you stopped for her."

"Kera," I replied.

"Kera. I knew that if this thing could catch your attention, then maybe it could catch his. So I decided to invest, but I still needed to do more. I could tell she wouldn't take kindly to how I treated the other girls and longed for a loving family, so I used them to provoke her and, in return, provoke him."

"That night, with T," I said to myself.

"Yes. I figured he might be around. I didn't expect things to advance so quickly, though. I must admit he took her sooner that what I would have liked, but it was not outside of my expectations. After that, the only thing left to determine was whether that man was telling the truth or not."

"Man?" I asked.

"Let's call him a friend."

"That night with the guards, it was you."

"I knew you would take a liking to I, that you would come here every night. All I had to do was simply encourage the men of this town to go pay your lord a visit when you just happened to be away."

"You planned this ... all of it!"

"Of course. You don't take on a creature like the lord or even yourself without preparation. I waited for a night when you were gone and sent Marcus and his men in. It wasn't hard. I promised Marcus Kera as the spoils of war—something he had wanted for a long time. And as for his men, I simply promised them a free drink to slay a beast. They were my way of finding whether my suspicions were correct."

"That's impossible! They were all killed that night; there was no one left alive to report back to you," I explained.

"Ah, yes, I was not expecting your little friend; he was a surprise. After the incident, Marcus met with me in the woods nearby to tell me what had transpired. He managed to tell me everything before I saw your friend in the distance. Marcus bravely volunteered to stay behind so I could escape without him even knowing I was there. I knew everything I needed about your lord."

"Those weapons."

"Like I said, Mr Butler, a friend."

"What friend? What's his name!" I demanded.

"That I cannot tell you, but he does know of you, of the lord, and of a great number of many other things."

"I don't understand; why do all of this? Why hurt I or tell me any of this? You're not strong enough to fight him, and if your plan is to use me, then it won't work; even I am no match for him at full strength."

"But he isn't at full strength, is he. I know he is weak, and without you by his side, he is even weaker."

"Reno will—"

"Reno will be too busy with you, though." He snickered.

"What do you mean? The lord will know I'm missing."

"Will he now? But didn't you tell him you would be here during the night? That you couldn't accompany him? That you would be with T?"

"You little ..."

"The lord has no reason to look for you, and Kera will think T is safe with you. Both she and the lord will be far too busy with one another. As for your friend Reno, he will simply follow Beth like a love-struck puppy. I heard how he has become attached."

"Even if that is the case, how do you possibly plan on killing him?"

"Killing him? What makes you think I want to kill him?"

"You can't ... The chances of it succeeding—"

"I know my chances and happen to have a little something to tip the odds in my favour. If I were you, I would worry less about the lord and more about her. The poison works fast; she has a few hours at best."

With that he walked past me to leave.

"Wait. The antidote," I begged.

"Not to worry, Mr Butler; I will send someone within the hour with the antidote. In the meantime, keep your word and stay here."

"Why don't I just kill you and save her myself."

He walked over to me as I was knelt, caring for T. He lifted my chin with his fingers firmly and leaned into my ear and whispered softly. "Because you need me." He leaned back, still holding my chin. "Look how much stronger you are than I, yet how powerless you are, all over a woman ... pathetic."

After he left, my attention turned immediately to T. I scooped her up and carried her to Tarell's room. There where chains on the bed, and equipment of all kinds lay scattered about. It appeared to be doctors' tools, and I knew quickly what had happened here. Blood trailed behind us from the cellar to the room, creating a blanket of red as we went. Once on the bed, I ripped down one of the curtains, creating bits of cloth, and gathered some water from downstairs to clean her up. By the time I was done, there were so many wounds that almost every inch of her body was wrapped in red cloth like a gift. I lay beside her, stroking her hair, and she began to come around. Still weak, she spoke.

"Mr Butler."

"I'm here."

"Sorry I can't go with you to the ball."

"No, I'm sorry. I promised to keep you safe, and I failed again. I failed to—"

"It's okay; it's not your fault. You're not responsible for the actions of others."

"You remind me of her so much."

"Of who?"

"Someone I knew, she was small and, like you, seemed like she would break with the slightest touch. She had this presence about her that just made everyone around her light up. She could bring joy and light to any situation. She was my ray of sunshine, and I loved her very much. Then one day something happened; I wasn't able to make it to her in time, and I lost her. I failed her as I have failed you. And what's worse is that in her final moments she smiled up at me and simply thanked me. I still don't know why."

"I do; you came for her. You were there for her like you promised, meaning she wasn't alone in the end."

I couldn't help it; tears started to fall down my face.

"Shh, it's okay. I'm not alone; I'm with you. You kept your promise to me as well. It's okay, really ... I never thought I would be so lucky as to have someone care for me like you do. Thank you, Mr Butler."

"Ray . . . my name is Ray."

"Like the sun; it's perfect."

"She thought so also when she gave it to me."

With that her eyes closed once more, and I could hear her heartbeat growing fainter by the second. I couldn't do anything other than hold her close and lie with her, praying that someone, anyone, would come.

The Night of the Ball

10 October 1836

After my long session with the lord, night had come about and the ball was about to start. I was excited, at first, to get all dressed up and dance under the lights, but that isn't what happened. A night that should have been full of music and wonder quickly turned into a night of horror.

As I woke up, I could see the lord was already dressed and ready for the ball, waiting patiently by my side.

"Morning," he said.

"Not quite," I replied with a smile. "What time is it?"

"Time for the ball. Our guests have already started to arrive, so I think it best if we join them."

"Or we could stay here," I suggested, seductively patting the bed.

He laughed and walked over to me. I was still naked, with only a sheet barely covering my naked form.

"As tempting as that is," he said, moving his hand up my leg, "we cannot be rude to our guests." His hand once again started to wrap around my throat. "Besides"—he squeezed hard—"if I were to start again, I would be afraid I could not stop." He kissed me, biting my upper lip before letting go.

I let out a disgruntled groan; I could already feel myself getting wet again. I got out of the bed and saw he had brought my clothes into his room, and I began to change. He watched me as I did. Once done, he walked over to me with the necklace he had got me from the jewellery shop and placed it around my neck. It was two rings—simple in design, silver with blue stones—on a silver chain. One had half a heart, and the other ring the other half; it was beautifully elegant.

"One of the rings is mine, but if I were to wear mine, it could put you in danger, so I want you to wear it for me. With it, know that my heart, if you will accept it, belongs to you now."

"Nothing would make me happier."

With that he pulled me in for one last passionate kiss before we headed downstairs to the ball. Along the way, we saw Reno with Beth; she looked stunning, and Reno also looked very handsome. She was wearing the bracelet that Reno had got her; it had three little flower charms dangling from it: one small lily, a hydrangea, and a white rose. I found out later that the three flowers represented us three girls; it was a way for Beth to keep us with her at all times.

We met at the stairs and decided to head down together. Beth and Reno led. Guests were arriving one after another. I stood by the lord's side as we greeted them, and I bowed to our guests as they bowed to the lord.

The ball was soon in full swing; there were men and women that I had never seen before; I doubt they were all from our town. Dressed in beautiful gowns and fancy suits, all of the gentlemen and ladies looked so refined. The hall was sparkling, the music soothing as people danced in unison to it.

For the first part of the evening, all eyes were shifting onto me and the lord, with whispers echoing around the room. I enjoyed the sight in front of me, but it was quickly ruined by a voice from the left. I saw my brother arrive late with Charlotte on his arm. I could tell it was not by his choice. He saw me and smiled, but we didn't get chance to exchange greetings, as Charlotte quickly pulled him away to mingle with the guests.

As the night went on, I had yet to see T or Ray, and I started to grow concerned. I expressed my worries to the lord, who assured me that she would be fine as long as Ray was with her. He said that I should enjoy the night and that she would turn up before I knew it. One after another, the guests formally introduced themselves to us and engaged in small talk. For the most part, I kept quiet, as I was embarrassed. I slipped away from the lord to take a break from the mingling, as I wasn't overly keen on people owing to past events. I sneaked away into a less crowded space and stood quietly at one of the windows, looking for T, until a gentleman came over to me. He was very tall with a slim but toned build, dressed all in white with long blond hair and yellow eyes. He took my hand and kissed it gently as he bowed. I curtsied back and smiled politely, my eyes fixed outside.

"Expecting someone?" he asked. "All of the guests have arrived already."

"Oh, my friend is yet to turn up, so I was just ..." I took a breath. "I'm sorry; I am being rude. It's a pleasure to meet you."

"Sebastian," he replied. "And likewise. I am sure your friend will turn up. But, in the meantime, if I could be so bold as to ask for this dance." He stretched out his arm as an invitation.

I looked over to see that Reno and Beth were already dancing. How Reno had managed that I was not sure, but I could see how happy they were. I looked over to the lord and saw that he seemed busy in conversation with some men, so I accepted Sebastian's offer.

"I apologize in advance, but I am afraid I am not a very good dancer," I said.

"Don't worry, Kera; I am. Just follow me and everything will be fine."

With that he took me to the centre of the room, and as he had said, he guided me the entire time. His movements were flawless. It was as thought I wasn't even dancing but was floating gracefully. I couldn't help but smile; this man could move so well, and it was fun. As we continued to dance, people began to stop and stare in appreciation. I closed my eyes, enjoying the dance, until I felt a strong tug pull me back to my senses. The lord had pulled me into his chest and had no intention of letting go. He looked at Sebastian in a way that gave me chills. I got the impression Sebastian was not someone the lord liked.

"It's been a while," said Sebastian. "How have you been?"

The lord did not reply; he simply kept his gaze on Sebastian and tightened his grip on me more. Both of them were locked in a gaze. I dared not move a muscle. The silence was broken by a group of older men calling the lord over.

"Don't you have business to attend to?" asked Sebastian. "Don't worry; we are only dancing. I will return her straight after. Besides, she seemed to be enjoying herself." He looked at me. "Were you not?"

I could see that the waiting men were getting impatient; whatever they wanted the lord for seemed important.

"Go," I said to the lord. Then I turned to Sebastian and curtseyed. "I did enjoy the dance, thank you, but I think I will go check in on my friend."

"I thought they had yet to arrive?" Sebastian asked.

"My other friend." I looked for Beth but could not see her.

"The young lady accompanying Reno, you mean. I saw her go outside while we were dancing, probably for some fresh air. I can walk you over if you like?"

The lord's grip tightened once more.

"It's okay, but thank you," I said. I turned to face the lord. He looked almost troubled. I pulled him in for a gentle kiss and reassured him everything was okay.

"My apologies, Matt. I did not realize you were involved with Kera. And here I was, hoping we could dance some more. Never mind, I have my own matters to attend to. I hope your friend turns up." With that he bowed and walked away into the crowd.

The men were still eagerly awaiting the lord. Suddenly Reno came rushing up to us, saying it was important that the lord go speak with them immediately. I asked where Beth was, and he replied that she was outside and that he would be there soon. I insisted that the lord go speak with these men. I reassured him that I would be okay and went outside to find Beth. The lord, Reno, and the other men left the ballroom for the sitting room. Whatever the topic of discussion was must have been important. I got outside but couldn't find Beth anywhere. I began to walk around, heading for the garden in case she had taken a stroll. As I got there, I heard a voice from behind me that froze me in fear.

"My my, don't you look lovely."

I turned to see Tarell standing behind me, dressed in a black suit with a deep red shirt. Despite how much I hated this man, I had to admit he did look slightly bewitching. As he looked at me, he began to creep closer.

"I must admit, even for me, looking at you now, knowing I could take you, the temptation to do so is overwhelming," he said, now only a few inches from me. "I can see the lord didn't waste any time." He stroked my neck where a mark had been left from earlier. "I wonder if I bit hard enough whether I, too, could mark that beautiful pale skin of yours." He leaned in, his mouth open. I felt his breath on my neck and pushed him away before he could bite.

"What do you want? Why are you here? Where is T?" I snapped.

"So many questions, and after I have already answered so many for Beth."

"What?"

"Well, you see, she was here before you, and she, too, wanted to know many things, so I answered her. With that she got rather upset and headed for the tavern." He grinned.

"Upset? Why? What did you do?"

"Shouldn't you be more concerned about yourself? After all, it can't be easy dating a monster."

"How did you—"

"I know plenty, Kera, and a great deal more than you. Anyway, I advise you enjoy the ball."

"But Beth."

"What could I possibly do to her? She is on her way back to the tavern, and I am here. What threat do I pose?"

"I know you are up to something. I'm going—"

"Going to what? Abandon the lord? interrupt his ball? Embarrass him in front of all his guest?"

I knew he was right, and I didn't want to cause the lord any trouble. I also knew that sneaking off wasn't an option.

"Doesn't Beth have her own partner now for these kind of things? Speaking of which …"

With that I heard Reno's voice calling for Beth as he came closer towards us. Tarell winked at me and headed inside through the side door of the garden. I called Reno over. He too was looking for Beth. I explained to him that Tarell had informed me she had gone back to the tavern, but I did not know why. I saw his face fill with concern. With that he went after her and told me to return to the lord and try not to worry. Reluctantly, with a knot in my stomach, I agreed and returned to the ball to find the lord looking for me. When he saw me, he quickly rushed over with an expression of relief on his face. He asked whether

I was okay. I didn't tell him about Beth or Reno, as he seemed agitated. Instead I told him everything was fine and asked how he was. He smiled politely and tried to convince me he was okay, but I could see that wasn't the case.

"May I have this dance?" the lord asked. "I wanted the first one with you, but it seems I was beaten to it."

I lowered my head apologetically, and he lifted it back up. "I would love to dance," I replied.

With that we walked over to the centre of the room once again. Wrapped in his embrace, I simply moved with him as we danced together. The music filled the air. All I could smell was him; all I could feel was him. As I closed my eyes, I felt at home; and in that moment, nothing else mattered but us.

Beth's Encounter

10 October 1836

My heart was racing as I got closer to the tavern. I knew Tarell had done something to T, and as I got closer, my mind played out one horrific scenario after another. As I opened the tavern door, I could see a trail of blood leading upstairs. I followed it nervously, praying she was still alive. When I got upstairs to Tarell's bedroom and slowly creaked the door open in fear of what might greet me, I stood in disbelief as I saw a bloody and naked T in the arms of the butler.

"What did you do! Is she—?"

The butler slowly raised his head to look up at me. "No, not yet."

I let out a sigh of relief. "Wait, what do you mean, 'Not yet'? What is going on, and what did you do?"

"Do you really think I would do this?"

I paused for a moment. "Tarell."

"I came to collect her for the ball. When I did, I found her chained up in the cellar, dangling from a hook like a piece of meat."

My face turned white. I knew exactly what Tarell had done—what it felt like.

"I treated her wounds as best I could," he continued, "But Tarell poisoned her and told me to wait here for someone to bring the antidote. If I were to leave, she would die."

"Why isn't the lord looking for you?"

"I made a deal with Tarell before the ball; he would let T go only if I were to come back here during the ball to check on the tavern to ensure it was safe. The lord knows this and expects me to be absent. Tarell set up the whole thing so as not to raise alarms."

"Wait ... antidote ... *Reno!*"

"Reno? What does he have to do with this?"

"Now it makes sense."

"What does?"

"The night the lord turned and we saw what you were for the first time, Reno came to my room. As we spoke, I lost my temper and ended up smashing one of the vases, cutting my hand. Reno calmed me down and treated the wound. When he was doing so, he said there was something strange about it. I let him taste it, and he said that it was tainted with something, like an antidote. He said it was the result of a substance being introduced into my system slowly over the years. I figured it was just Tarell securing his assets, but could he really have been planning this all this time?"

"Wait, you're telling me your blood could cure her?" he asked me, his eyes hopeful.

"I don't know, but we need to try."

"The amount of poison in her system is not small. Based on how fast it is working, I will need to take quite a bit," he explained.

"Take what you need, but do it quickly," I said as I rushed to the bed to lie beside her. "The longer we wait, the worse her chances are."

"Very well, but there is no easy way to do this. I will have to cut into your wrist and feed it directly into her mouth; it will be the quickest way." He pulled out a blade near his waist.

"I understand. Do it, and don't stop until she wakes up!"

"Beth, this could—"

"I know ... Now get on with it; you're wasting time."

With that I closed my eyes and handed my wrist over to the butler. I took a deep breath as I felt the cold knife up against my wrist. A sharp pain hit me, and I could feel the blood begin to drain. As he placed my wrist on T's lips, he squeezed gently, forcing the blood out quicker. Not long after he started, I could already feel myself slipping out of consciousness. As he squeezed again, I prayed that this would work.

The butler paused for a moment. "This will help," he said as he pulled out a small vial and poured a few drops of a red liquid into my mouth. Within seconds I could feel myself coming back, though I was still dizzy and unable to move. I heard footsteps downstairs, and a familiar voice called out my name. Moments later, I saw Reno standing at the door.

"Ray, what have you done!" said Reno as he stood there horrified.

"I did nothing to either of them; it was Tarell. Beth is—" The butler was interrupted by a deep growl.

"Let her go! *Now!*" Reno snarled.

"I Can't!"

"*Now*, Ray! Before I rip your throat out!"

"I can't! Just let me explain!"

With that Reno leapt at Ray in a blind rage. Ray put his hands up in time to brace for most of the impact, but it still knocked me back hard, splitting the wall behind me. Ray climbed back to his feet, his rage building. He lunged, shoving Reno hard across the room into the furniture, smashing it to pieces. Ray returned to us and resumed the treatment, but as he did, part of a chair came flying towards him. He moved to dodge, but Reno charged up behind him, grabbed him, and threw him roughly over his shoulder and out the room, near the top of the stairs. As Ray got back to his feet, Reno charged like a bull. Ray sidestepped at the last second, grabbing Reno by the hair and using his momentum to swing him back into the bedroom with such force that Reno's body not only cracked the wall but also shook the entire building. Ray slowly walked back towards the room, brushing dust off his shirt.

"Stay down, Reno, for your own sake," Ray said calmly as he walked back into the room.

"You know I won't do that!" Reno replied, climbing back to his feet, spitting out blood from the impact.

"I promise you I am not hurting either of them, but if you don't get out of my way, I will not continue to hold back. You know you are not strong enough to beat me."

"I don't know, maybe it's my lucky day." With that Reno charged once more. He swung over and over again, desperately trying to land a hit on Ray, but with no luck. The difference in their power was clear as Ray easily moved from side to side, avoiding Reno's attacks. After a few minutes of Reno struggling desperately, Ray landed one punch into his stomach. I could hear bones breaking, and Reno curled over and fell to the floor.

"Please," Ray said. "Stay down."

"You may be stronger," Reno replied, gasping for air, "but even you aren't immune."

With that I saw a look of horror creep onto Ray's face as he stared back at Reno. I knew about Reno's ability to hypnotize others, but I didn't know whether it worked on his own kind. It wasn't fully effective, as I could see Ray struggling, but it was effective enough to give Reno a fighting chance. Reno rushed him quickly, telling Ray to stop. With Ray unable to defend himself, Reno was finally able to land a hit. Over and over he danced around Ray, striking blow after blow so quickly it was hard to keep up with them. I could hear Reno's punches and kicks as they echoed throughout the room. He rained down hit after hit until Ray was finally knocked to the floor. In seconds, Reno had climbed on top of him, his hands around his throat, squeezing the life out of him. Ray was unable to get free, and he struggled desperately to speak.

"Reno," Ray struggled to say as he gasped for air. "You don't understand."

"No, *you don't!*" Reno shouted. "No wonder you couldn't protect your sister."

I didn't know anything about Ray's past, but I knew that Reno had made a grave mistake. Ray's eyes filled with rage, his body tensed, and he seemed to have gotten a lot stronger. I could see the fear in Reno's face; desperately he tried to tighten his grip, but it was no use. Ray pushed Reno off him with ease using only the palm of his hand, sending Reno flying back, the wall taking yet another hit. Ray calmly got to his feet and slowly approached Reno, his eyes wide and shining yellow. Reno tried to scamper away, but it was no use; Ray was already towering over him. He reached out his hand and placed it around Reno's throat, slowly lifting him off the ground and into the air. Reno kicked desperately to try and escape, but it was in vain. Ray simply stood there, a cold look on his face, as he took his time squeezing the life out of Reno breath by breath. As Reno began to fade, I tried to speak, to move, to do anything to make them stop, but all I could do was watch. I thought Reno was about to die until I head a small voice cry out from beside me.

"Please stop."

I turned to see that T had come to, tears trickling down her face.

I turned back to see Ray frozen in place. After a few seconds, he released his grip on Reno and rushed to T's side.

"You're okay?" he asked.

"Yes, I am ... *Watch out!*"

Ray turned just in time to see Reno rush him with a sharp piece of broken wood, but he wasn't able to move in time; Reno had once again locked his eyes with Ray, forcing him to remain still long enough for Reno to drive the wood fully through Ray's chest. Blood splattered everywhere, painting the room red. Reno let go of the wood and backed away slowly.

Ray turned to face T once more. "I am glad you are okay," he said softly, and he then fell to the floor.

"*Rayyyy!*" T screamed as she fell out of the bed and crawled beside him. "What have you done!" she yelled at Reno.

"He was ... I mean ... I was trying ..." he started to say.

"He didn't do anything. It was *Tarell!* He poisoned me! Ray was trying to *save* me! I heard Beth say to Ray that she had an antidote in her blood. They were *saving me!*"

"But I thought—"

"You thought wrong!"

"Ray ... what have I done?"

Reno quickly rushed to his side but was blocked by T.

"*Stay away!*" she demanded

Reno stood in place, helpless. Like a lost child, he didn't know what to do. I knew I needed to do something, so I mustered up all of the strength I had left and was able to speak.

"Reno," I said quietly, "you need to help him."

He looked over to me, his eyes full of tears.

"T, you need to let Reno help; he is the only one who can."

"No! No, I'm not letting—"

"T! Please ... He didn't know, but if you don't want Ray to die, then let him help now, and be mad later."

She looked at me and then at Reno. I had never seen that expression on her before. A look of hate and anger, it made her seem like a completely different person.

"Fine," she snapped.

Reno rushed over to Ray, placed his head on his knees, and bit hard into his own wrist.

"What are you doing?" T asked.

"He has lost a lot of blood; he needs more to recover, otherwise he might ..."

"Then use mine. I can—"

"You are far too weak; it would kill you. Besides, Ray isn't like the rest of us. He needs something stronger than human blood."

"Tarell," Ray said, pulling Reno in close. "He is up to something. Don't underestimate him; don't make the same mistake I did." With that Ray went silent.

"Ray ... Ray, you said you wouldn't leave me, remember?" T cried.

"And he won't," Reno stated to T as he ripped a chunk of flesh off his wrist and placed the gushing wound over Ray's mouth.

"Why? Why did he try to save me?" T cried.

"He wanted keep his promise," Reno explained. "A long time ago, he made a promise to someone that he couldn't keep. He has never forgiven himself, not for a second. Maybe with you he saw his chance to finally keep that promise."

Ray had slowly started to come to but was still very weak; he could see Reno struggling with his own blood loss.

"Reno," Ray said, "you need to stop. if you do not, then you will pass out and there will be no one to protect the girls or the lord. You can't risk—" Ray began to protest.

"I'm fine Ray," Reno argued. "Just a bit more, then I will get everyone downstairs to the cellar so you're safe and head back to the ball for the lord."

"Reno, you are not strong enough to—"

"Yes I am. I may not be as strong as you, Ray, but that doesn't mean I am weak."

With that Reno pulled his wrist away from Ray and quickly bandaged it up. Staggering, he got to his feet and walked over to me. He looked pale, as if he was about to collapse at any moment, but he didn't stop. He scooped me up and proceeded downstairs to the cellar. He gently laid me down and left, returning only a few minutes later with Ray and T following slowly behind. T had recovered from the poison but was still barely able to move.

As he placed Ray down, Reno fell with him, both of them unconscious. I knew I had no strength to move, and neither did T. All we could do now was hope that someone would come save us. T sat beside Ray and placed his head on her lap, gently stroking his hair.

"Beth, I don't know what's going on, and I don't need to know," T said, not taking her eyes off Ray. "But everything is going to be okay, right?"

"Don't worry, T," I assured her, "they are a lot stronger than they look. Before you know it will be out of here, safe and away from this place for good."

BAIT

10 OCTOBER 1836

My concern started to grow more and more. Over an hour had passed since Reno had left. Tarell was still here, but I couldn't shake the feeling that something had gone wrong. I saw Tarell leave from across the room. Curious, I followed. The lord was still speaking to Sebastian, as he didn't really give him much of a choice when he insisted on speaking in private. I looked back at the lord. I wanted to call for him, but Tarell's words rang in the back of my mind and I continued.

I followed Tarell outside, where a carriage was waiting for him. Desperate to follow, I sneaked onto the back before it set off. I had an idea of where we were going, and I was right; we soon arrived at the tavern. I waited for him to go inside before I approached. As I did, I could see the walls had cracks running down them. The entire building looked as though it had been shaken by the earth itself. I creaked the door open slowly and didn't see any signs of Tarell, but I did see a large trail of blood, one part of it leading upstairs and one to the cellar. My heart sunk as I tried to figure out whose it was and feared the worst. I approached the cellar, and as I did, something hit me hard from behind, knocking me unconscious. When I came to, my arms were bound behind my back. Like the first time Tarell and I had met, he had me in front of him like a human shield, with a tight grip on the rope. He was standing patiently, waiting, facing towards the door. It didn't take me long to realize who he was waiting for.

"The lord," I muttered under my breath.

"Oh, you're awake," said Tarell. "And just in time. He will be here soon."

"Whatever it is you are planning, it won't work; you're not strong enough to—"

"Oh, I know," he interjected. "That's why I have you, as well as some extra insurance if I need it."

"Why are you doing this? Why now?"

"It was years ago; I was catering to a stranger in the tavern and had forgotten about one of my girls. I didn't realize it, but some of the men had sneaked her out back to have their way. I realized soon after, and as I went outside to check, I saw a monster with wings as black as night sinking its teeth into the neck of one of the men as the bodies of the others lay torn to shreds on the ground. Frozen with fear, I could not move. Then I heard a voice call out, 'My Lord!' Seconds later, this monster had turned into a man. He walked towards the girl, ignoring the corpses he had just made, but the girl was already dead. He left with the butler. I checked the girl to be sure, and she was indeed dead. Later that night, I buried the bodies and hid all evidence of what had happened. I waited for this man to return, thinking I would be next, but he never did. I learnt over time with a little bit of help who he was. The only man who fitted that description was your *lord*. So I began to think, 'What if I had that power? The things I could achieve would be limitless."

"You planned all of this so you could become a vampire?"

"Is that what they call themselves? Ever since that day, that monster has haunted my every dream. So much power in one man. I wanted it, but I knew I would never stand a chance against that thing, so instead I focused on the man instead. The way he reacted over the girl that night, I could see the despair in his face. I found it strange that he would care so much for a stranger, so at first I thought maybe he knew her, but later on I found out that he had lost someone. I knew love would be his weakness. Then, when I saw him look at you the way he did in town that day, I knew I had found my way in."

"You used me just to get to him?"

"Why else would I take any intertest in you. There were some unexpected events. Originally my plan was simply to take you and exchange your life for his, but I didn't expect Beth to fight back. I guess she never did get over the death of her friend and was making up for it with you two. Nor did I expect for the lord to have a guest turn up. Lucky for me, it seems the butler fell for T, and the lord's guest for Beth. All of them are blinded by love, making them easy to manipulate."

"What did you do to them? Where are they?" I demanded.

"Don't worry; they are around. All I needed to do was set up events so everything would play out accordingly. Timing was key. I had to get all of you alone. You three girls weren't an issue, but the lord's butler and his unexpected guest were. However, thanks to the charms of the three of you, it was easier than I had thought. After that, everything had to time out just right, and those involved needed to play their parts precisely. And they did; you all outperformed my expectations, doing exactly what I wanted." He let out a hearty laugh.

"You don't understand. He can't give you his power; it will more than likely kill you. So all of this …"

"I know how it works, but I have something to tip the odds in my favour. All I need now is for him to show up."

"He will kill you before—"

"No he won't. He wouldn't dare do anything that would hurt you, and even if he did, I'm sure you wouldn't want your friends to die. Would you?"

"What do you mean?"

"Beneath our very feet are your friends. It seems there was a misunderstanding and both the butler and the little red-headed one got hurt. Of course, I know they can recover over time, so to be safe, the tavern is rigged with gunpowder. If it were to go off with your friends trapped downstairs, I doubt they would survive." He grinned.

"You bastard!" I shouted. As I struggled to turn, he secured his grip tighter and pulled me hard against his chest, he pulled a blade out and placed it across my throat. As he did, the door flew open so hard it came off its hinges and smashed into little pieces against the back wall. Standing there was the lord, eyes pitch black, already fully transformed, his body filling the doorway.

"I wouldn't. I know you can easily kill me, but not before I slit her throat. I may not be able to hurt you, but I can easily hurt her," said Tarell as he pushed down on the blade, cutting slightly into my neck. "Now change back."

The lord let out a low growl as he stopped moving and eased his gaze. Like a dog accepting a command, he changed back to his human form, his eyes still pitch black.

"Good boy," Tarell said sarcastically.

A sudden outburst of soft cries came vibrating through the tavern floor from beneath us; it sounded like someone calling for help.

"It seems like they are running out of time. I wonder how long they will last until one of them bleeds out. More importantly, back to us."

"What is it you want?" asked the lord.

"That night, when you slaughtered those men—"

"So you were watching me."

"I want that power. Give me it, and I will let her and your friends go. Kill me, they will all die."

"Not if I kill you first," the lord snarled.

"True. But you're not at full strength, are you? Even if you saved her, could you save them as well? Do you think she will forgive you—the monster who killed her only ever family—for being the reason why her friends are dead?"

I opened my mouth to speak, but Tarell's hand covered it before any sound came out.

"You give me what I want, and I will return what you want."

"It doesn't always work."

"I will take my chances. Now what do you say, *my Lord?*"

He looked at me and then bowed his head in defeat. "Fine, I will do as you ask, but as soon as you are turned …"

"Oh, not here. I know the second I start to turn, you will simply kill me. I also know how it works. Take this." With that he threw a vial to the lord. "Fill it with the amount needed for a turn, and I will do the rest myself once I am safe."

Reluctantly the lord took the vial. It was designed so that as he bit into the top, what looked like venom dripped from his fangs into the vial, filling it up drop by drop. Once he was done, he demanded that Tarell release me.

"But of course. Now, if you would be so kind," Tarell said, holding his hand out for the vial. "Just pass it to Miss Stone here; no need for you to get too close."

The lord approached me and handed me the vial. He smiled as if to assure me everything would be okay. Tarell used me as a shield to get to the door. I knew that if Tarell was to escape now, I would never be free of him—that this demon would come back. As he got closer to the door, I took a deep breath and turned suddenly to face Tarell, using all of my strength to push us both down. I felt the blade slice across my throat as I did, along with the warmth of my own blood quickly flowing down my neck, but I knew I had given the lord the window he needed to fight back.

The lord was instantly in front of me and in one fell swoop lifted Tarell into the air.

"You want my venom so badly? Fine, then take it!" he growled, and with that he sunk his teeth deep into Tarell's neck. Blood squirted out, spraying the walls, as he began to drain him. Within moments Tarell's body went limp, his eyes dark and his face white. The lord tossed Tarell to one side like rubbish and came rushing over to me. The cut on my throat was deep, and the bleeding wasn't slowing.

"Its going to be okay," assured the lord as he quickly ripped a bit of cloth of his shirt to stem the bleeding. "I promise it's—"

"Downstairs ... Beth, T ... the cellar ... you need to ..." I said as I felt my body becoming cold.

"Shh, it's okay; I will get them. I will save you. Everything will be okay."

"Please ... save them," I begged.

"But I need to save you. I can't go back to a life without you. Please, I don't want to lose anyone again; I don't want to lose you," he whimpered as he placed his head against mine.

"You won't lose me. You might not be able to see me, but that doesn't mean you will forget me. You gave me a life—showed me what it was to be happy, to be respected ... to be loved. The short time I spent with you was the best time of my life—more than I could ever ask for. Now let me save you; let me save them ... like you saved me. The tavern is rigged with gunpowder; you don't have time to get us all."

He squeezed my hand tight before whispering into my ear. "I could turn you; you're going to die if I don't."

"No."

"But why not? It—"

"Because I won't have you watch me suffer," I interrupted. "You said the chances of it working are very low; I won't have you watch me die twice."

"Please don't make me watch you die once," he pleaded.

With that I felt a sudden gust of wind hit us hard, and there was a loud bang. I managed to turn my head to see Tarell standing with a torch in his hand; he had set the gunpowder alight, and in an instant the whole tavern had gone up in a blaze. The ceiling began to give, the stairs lay broken, and flames started to engulf the tavern. He stood over the cellar door as smoke began seep through.

"What will you do now?" Tarell said, his eyes a deep green. "You can't save them all. Thank you for my gift; I know you injected a lethal amount into my body, hoping to kill me painfully, but instead you just made me stronger."

"How?" the lord asked "That much should have killed you even if you were compatible."

"I guess I got lucky," he growled.

Tarell did not move; he locked his eyes with the lord's. "Your move, *my Lord.*"

The lord looked at me, took a deep breath, and apologized. Seconds later, I felt his teeth pierce my neck. Tarell did not move; he simply watched as I felt his venom flowing into me. My body finally gave up on me, and I fell into a deep sleep, hoping I would wake to see him again.

The lord's Battle

10 October 1836

"You will pay for this!" I snarled, taking my true form. "Once I have killed you, am going to take her if she lives. I will devour her in every way I can and keep her purely for my entertainment. As for you and your friends, I will burn the lot of you together!"

Tarell leapt forward, fangs bared, pouncing like a predator through the flames, aiming for my neck. I caught him in mid-air and threw him hard against the tavern wall, bringing part of the ceiling down on top of him.

"You may have succeed in turning, but you are still weak! I have thousands of years on you, boy!"

Tarell burst out of the rubble, pouncing for a second attack. This time as I went to grab him, he seemed to simply vanish into the air. Then I suddenly felt him on my back. Before I had a chance to grab him, his claws dug deep into my shoulders. Riding my back, he once again went for my neck. I blocked with my hand, wrapping it around Tarell's mouth and hurling him hard onto the floor, sending him across the room through the burning rubble.

I walked across the room and pulled Tarell up by the throat. My body had begun to feel strange, and I knew he had done something to me.

"What have you done to me?" I demanded, my claws digging into his throat.

Laughing, Tarell replied, "It looks like my new-found change came with a little perk."

"You have an ability?"

"And you are out of time, my Lord," he stated, looking at the cellar.

In the heat of the battle, I had forgotten about the others. I released Tarell and darted over to the cellar door to rescue them. Tarell quickly scurried away. I forced open the cellar door to see all of them unconscious under the smoke. Ray and Reno were both badly hurt. I called out desperately to them, but I was quickly interrupted. Tarell had come rushing back, swiping at me like a wild bear, forcing me away from the cellar as I dodged his attacks.

I was stronger, but he appeared to be quicker. As I tried to fight back, I couldn't land a hit. He dodged my strikes over and over. Each time, he was able to counter with an attack of his own. After a number of blows, I fell to my knees, already weak from before with multiple gashes. I was losing a lot of blood. He stood in front of me triumphantly, getting ready to deliver the final blow, and that's when I saw his eyes; they had the same look to them as Reno's. As he raised his hand high into the air, ready to rip out my throat, I closed me eyes. I felt the air move as he went to strike. Inches from my neck,

I grabbed his hand. Keeping my eyes closed, I rose to my feet, crushing the bone. He let out a blood-curdling scream of pain, and I released my grip. I kicked him hard and felt his ribs break under my boot. The impact sent him flying across the room, smashing into the wall on the other side, bringing yet more of the ceiling down. I could hear him gasping for air as I approached; he was frantically trying to get up. As I got close, I bared my teeth. This time it was I who was going to deliver the killing blow.

"How?" he coughed. "How did you know?"

"That look in your eyes. It is very similar to Reno's. Only one man is faster than me, and it is not you! Meaning that what I was seeing had to be a hallucination—making me think you were in once place, when in reality you were not. It gives the illusion of speed but it is just that, an illusion, no real power of your own."

Tarell laughed, coughing up blood. "You might be strong, but are they?"

With that I suddenly took notice of my surroundings and saw the flames relentlessly consuming the tavern, the ceiling about to cave, the walls crumbling in front of my very eyes. The tavern was about to come down at any moment. I looked back to see that Kera had still not moved, and the flames begin to crawl downstairs into the cellar. Distracted, Tarell saw his chance and took it. He pulled out a black-tipped blade he had been concealing and plunged it straight into my chest. I felt it pierce my cell, and I fell instantly to the floor.

"He said this would work," Tarell bragged as he circled around me. "Now you can die alone like a monster should."

He lifted the dagger up with both hands, ready to plunge it into my chest once more. I looked to Kera in what I thought would be my final moments, praying that she would survive this. As I turned back and saw the dagger coming down, I suddenly saw two figures appear from behind Tarell.

"He is not alone," said Ray breathlessly.

"He has us," Reno added.

They had both wrapped their hands around his, stopping the dagger.

"What! No! You're supposed to be dead!" Tarell raged.

"We made a promise," said Ray.

"The girls would be mad if we died now," Reno explained.

"You!" Tarell stared at Ray. "How could you possibly recover?"

"With help from a friend," Ray answered.

With both of them still weak, they worked together, pulling Tarell back. As if dancing, they moved around him, taking turns striking blows at Tarell, not giving him a chance to gain his balance or even react. Finally they stuck the final blow together in unison, aiming hard at his cell. I heard a loud crack as their fists impaled Tarell's chest, forcing his cell out of his body. Tarell quickly turned as white as a ghost as his body began to wither. In the few seconds he had left to live, he turned to face me one last time.

"I am not the only one," he asserted as he crumpled to the floor.

Reno rushed over to me as Ray headed downstairs to the cellar. He came back up not long after with T in his arms.

"Matt ... Matt, are you okay?" Reno asked, blood still dripping from his wounds.

"I'm okay. Get the girls out of here before this entire place falls down."

"Reno, take Kera, then come back for the lord; I will grab Beth," Ray commanded as he left with T.

Reno agreed, and he took Kera outside to safety. Ray returned for Beth. As he came back, a desperate hand grabbed at his ankle and plunged a dagger through it. Ray let out a scream of pain, collapsing to the floor. Seconds later, the tavern entrance finally gave, trapping everyone else inside.

"If am dying, I am taking as many with me as I can," Tarell panted as he dragged his rapidly decaying body over to Ray. Still grasping the black-tipped blade, he aimed for Ray's chest with the last of his strength.

"Nooooo!" I shouted, still unable to move.

As the dagger came down, a body suddenly blocked its path, throwing itself on top of Ray, acting as a shield.

"Impossible!" Tarell gasped.

The body staggered to its knees, but Tarell's blade still plunged into its back, forcing him to release his grip. "I won't let you hurt them any more!" Beth declared. She looked Tarell straight in the eyes. "You lose, Tarell." With that Tarell's body finally gave up on him as the last of his life left. Beth knelt there motionless before she spoke through blood-filled lungs.

"Take care of them for me," she spluttered, and her eyes shut as she began to fall to the ground. Ray caught her before she collapsed, but she was quickly dying. I mustered up the little strength I had left. I refused to watch us die here. I managed to get to my feet and stagger over to Ray. I told him to hold on to her tightly as I gripped him by the waist. I spread my wings as wide as they would go. With all the strength I could muster, I pushed hard off the ground and burst through the tavern roof, causing it to collapse completely out into the open sky. I didn't have the strength to fly, but I glided down as best I could, releasing Ray close to the ground with Beth still in his arms as I crashed down beside them.

Reno came rushing over immediately. He could see Beth was hurt.

"What happened?" Reno asked, sounding panicked.

"She saved my life," Ray replied.

"What do I ... I mean, what do I do?" he asked frantically.

"Take ... a ... chance," I said. "She's strong; she will survive."

"But I have never ... I didn't even think I could. I thought you had to ..." Reno said.

"I can't ... not like this. And she has only minutes left; you need to try," I told him.

With that he took Beth gently into his arms. Crying, he whispered that he was sorry into her ear and bit down as gently as he could. As he did, I saw Ray stumble over to T, who was still unconscious. He checked her pulse and then came to me.

"I think it is time we go home, sir," he said.

"Kera?" I asked.

"She is alive, but we can't stay here any longer; a crowd will gather soon. It will be okay. Reno and I will take care of everything."

With that I couldn't hold on any longer, and my eyes closed.

A NEW LIFE

12 OCTOBER 1836

I woke up as if from a dream, confused, not knowing what had really happened. I looked around to see a familiar sight; there was a small girl seated at my bedside with her head on my lap, asleep. Her cheeks were wet from tears. I knew then where I was. I gently woke my friend from her sleep. Overcome with joy, T threw herself into my arms, hugging me as tightly as she could. I did the same back. We stayed like that for a while before I asked her what had happened. She told me she didn't know and that the last thing she remembered was being in Tarell's cellar. After that, she said, she came to as she was on the back of a carriage and saw the tavern in a pile of rubble, destroyed. "What happened to everyone else?" I asked. "Is everyone okay?" She told me that everyone was okay, just badly injured, and that everyone but her was resting. I felt a wave of relief wash over me. She told me to go back to sleep and rest up.

Once I came to again, she was gone. This time the lord was sitting in her place.

"I see you're okay," I said.

"We're hard to kill," he replied.

The room fell silent, neither of us wanting to speak first. I took a deep breath and built up the courage to look at him. Nothing had changed. There were no scars, no wounds, no evidence that he had been in any kind of fight. All I could see through his open shirt was a small scar on his chest where his cell was.

"What happened?"

He looked at me, his eyes filled with regret. "I'm sorry. I couldn't. I just couldn't lose you. Not again."

"Again?"

"When Tarell … when he … I thought you were going to die, and I couldn't …" he was struggling to talk.

"This isn't the first time you have lost someone, is it?"

"No," he gently replied.

He told me a story from long ago. There was someone he loved, but he lost her during the war. He found her again but lost her to the cruelty of men. This continued to happen over the years; time after time, he lost her. After that, not wanting to go through the pain of losing her any more, he hid away, avoiding all human contact. It sounded like a curse: over the thousands of years he had been alive, every time he found the one he loved, she was taken away from him.

"I believe, Miss Stone, that death is not the end—that our bodies simply hold our souls until it is time for us to move onto another shell, where we get to start again. We may not have our memories, but our souls don't forget those we care for and find a way in each life to seek them out."

"What was her name?"

"It doesn't matter, what matters is I found you again, and you found me. I will say this to you once more: whether it be in this life or the next, no matter where you go, I will always find you, I will always be there for you, to love you, protect you, and give you everything you deserve."

I knew from the first few days I spent with him that I had fallen for this man but, if possible, I fell for him all over again. He was by far the best man I had ever met, strong and brave, kind, caring, loving—every good quality you could put into one person, he had. Most importantly, the people he cared about were his number-one priority.

I reached up to his face and pulled him in. "Thank you for finding me once more, my love."

With that we held each other tight. In his arms, I felt loved; it felt like home. After a few moments, I looked up to speak.

"I'm going to need a new name."

"Why?"

"Because the old me died in that tavern, with all the pain from the past. I would like to start a new life with you."

"What name were you thinking?"

"Hmm ... something simple and short."

"How about Jo?" he suggested.

"I like it."

"Kera ... I mean Jo ... there is one more thing I should mention."

"I know. I could tell as soon as I awoke. I'm not human any more, am I?"

"No. I'm sorry; it was the only way I could—"

"So instead of one lifetime with you, we get an eternity together."

A smile spread across his face with a sigh of relief. I could tell that he was worried—that in his mind maybe he had done the wrong thing. But for me it was a gift; I was given more time to be with the ones I loved, more time to be with him.

I asked him what would happen now, what I would do, and how I would live. He explained to me how often to feed. The amount of blood I would need to consume depended on how active I was. Much like when one's body is hungry and tells one to eat, the same principles apply. He warned me to be careful when feeding, as it is easy to get caught up in the moment and, with a seemingly unquenchable thirst, just keep drinking until the prey is dead. I asked whether I had to feed on humans, and he told me that animals would suffice, but as their blood is not the same as ours, it isn't as effective and won't last as long.

We talked at length for hours about how he lived and all the things I needed to know about being a vampire. When we were done, he got up and held out his hand for me.

"I thought vampires healed?" I asked, getting up and placing my hand on his chest. He noticed that the scars on my wrists were still there.

"Scars are not wounds that need healing, so even when your body turns, they remain. And if our kind is hurt badly enough, we cannot fully recover, leaving scars.

"Then let's make these the last ones," I stated.

We headed downstairs to where T and Ray were waiting patiently in the sitting room. T leapt to her feet and came rushing over, hugging us both.

"You're both okay," T said gleefully. "I was worried, Kera."

"Jo," I replied. "My name is Jo."

T paused for a moment. "I like it."

"Where are Beth and Reno?" I asked.

"They left," answered Ray.

"Left?"

"I own a small cabin not far from here," the lord explained. "They have gone there to figure things out. You are not the only one who changed."

"Wait, what? Beth? You mean she … but why … how?" I asked.

"By saving my life," Ray replied.

He then began to explain the events of the night to me. He told me everything that had happened with Tarell, himself, and Reno, and how Beth had saved his life. At first I was worried, but he assured me that she was happy, and if the end result meant that I didn't lose my friend, then I was okay with that.

"So they left so Beth could get accustomed to being a vampire?" I inquired.

"Yes," Ray said. "She recommend you do the same. She said she will come visit in a month or so, but until then she wants to be alone with Reno so she can learn to control it."

"And what about you?" I asked, turning towards T.

"Oh, I am good, thanks," she replied. "No offence, but I would rather not be a vampire; it seems like too much trouble."

"I meant what are you doing?"

"Ohhhhhh, I'm going with Ray. He is going to teach me how to fight, and I am going to keep an eye on him."

"Ray, you're leaving?" the lord said, sounding surprised.

"I'm afraid so, my Lord. Don't worry; we will not be far. And like Reno, I will return in a month's time. But if you need me before then, I will come. I would like to give her a chance at a normal life, and I wouldn't mind a slower pace myself for a change."

"Where will you go?" the lord asked.

"I'm not sure, but when we have found somewhere, I will let you know," Ray replied.

"Then come with me so we can prepare everything you need for your journey," the lord said, ushering him into the kitchen storage rooms.

"So it looks like we're all going our separate ways," T said.

"It would appear so," I answered

"Out of curiosity, I heard sometimes when you become a vampire you get some kind of cool power. What did you get?"

I chuckled. "I don't even know if I have one, but if I do, I promise you will be the first to know."

With that the lord came back with Ray, who had a bag on his shoulder. We all walked outside together, where a carriage was waiting.

"Well, Matthew, I guess I will see you soon," Ray said, happily extending his hand.

"I think that's the first time you have called me by my actual name," The lord replied, shaking Ray's hand.

"Jo." He bowed to me.

"Come here," I said, pulling him in for a hug. "Thank you, Ray, for everything."

"I already hugged you both, so bye, guys!" T shouted, skipping over to the carriage.

We saw them get on and watched as they rode away. When they were out of sight, we returned to an empty house.

"What now?" I asked.

"I have a few ideas," he whispered in my ear as his hand firmly grabbed my ass.

"Hmm," I whispered, leaning my body into his and nibbling at his ear. "Will you be okay?"

"Will you?" he whispered back, and with that he pushed me hard into the wall, lifting me up. I could already feel his erection against my stomach.

"let's see who gives first." I smiled, kissing him forcibly.

Beth's Vampire Training

13 November 1836

"It's going left!" Reno shouted.

"I see it. *It's mine!*" I replied as I lunged for the deer, pinning it to the ground and biting down hard on its neck.

"You're getting better at this, and it has only been a month," said Reno, catching me up.

"Strangely, it seems natural to me, as if I have just woken up to the real me."

"That's how I felt when I went through it."

"However," I said as she drained the last bit of life out of the deer, "there are so many things that don't add up about that night, meaning that what happened at the tavern is just the beginning. Considering what happened and what you have told me, something big is coming that won't involve just us but everyone from both sides."

"So that's why you wanted to come here—to train, to be ready, so you could protect them."

"I don't want be powerless or caught off guard ever again."

"If there is one thing I know about you, it is that you are not powerless," said Reno as he kissed me. "Besides, I'm here now."

"Yes, you are, and I'm grateful for it," I said, kissing Reno back. "Now shall we go say hello?"

"I suppose it has been a month. Besides, I know Ray will be missing me like crazy."

"I wonder how Kera is doing?"

"I wonder what her power is—that is, if she has one. Either way, it isn't going to be as cool as yours."

"Shall we go find out?" I asked.

Help from a Stranger

16 June 1839

"What are we going to do?" I asked. "There are too many bodies for us to hide, and they're on their way; we will be killed."

"I'm sorry. I'm so sorry, Beth," cried T. "I didn't mean to, I didn't ..."

"We will burn the place," I suggested. "Pile all the bodies up and burn everything. Then we run."

"*What?* But this is our home!" argued T.

"What choice do we have?"

We piled the bodies into the middle of the house and set it alight. As we fled, we stopped at a safe distance on top of a hill nearby to see the flames engulf our home. We took a moment, and then, as we went to leave, a tall man with long blond hair blocked our path.

"Good evening, ladies; it looks like you could do with some help."

"And you are?" I asked.

"Sebastian."

Milton Keynes UK
Ingram Content Group UK Ltd.
UKHW010704080823
426520UK00001B/161